**Nick Story Mysteries book two
A Killer of a Detail/Odd Jobs**

A Killer of a Detail

Nick is called because of a missing man. He went out in a boat with a mysterious woman and didn't come back.

Odd Jobs

An extremely handsome man finds a body in a flower bed.

Contents

A Killer of a Detail
Prologue   pg.   1
A Missing Person   pg.   4
You Have a Case   pg.   26
Boats and Cars   pg.   54
Solved!   pg.   79

Odd Jobs
The Job   pg.   87
A Clue or Two   pg.   93
Adding it Up   pg. 114
A Kid and a God   pg. 135
Solutions   pg. 156
Epilogue   pg. 177

About the Author

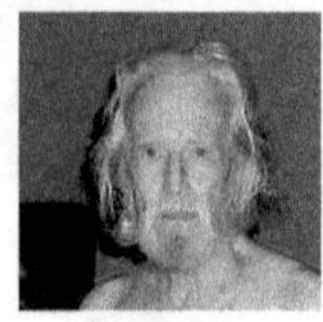

CD was born in Lakeland, Florida, in 1938. He is educated in genetics and botany. He has traveled over much of the world, particularly when he was in music as a rock rhythm guitarist with some well-known bands in the late sixties and early seventies. He has worked as a high steel worker and as a longshoreman, clerk, orchidist, bar owner, salvage yard manager and landscaper – among other things.

CD began writing fiction in 1984 and has more than 300 books published as of 3/15/16 in SciFi, murder, orchid culture and various other fields.

He now resides in Puerto Armuelles, David, and Gualaca, Chiriqui, Panamá, where he continues research into epiphytic plants and plays music with friends. He loves the culture of the indigenous people and counts a majority of his closer friends among that group. Several have "adopted" him as their father. He funds those he can afford through the universities where they have all excelled. "The Indios are very intelligent people, they are simply too poor (in material things and money. Culturally, they are very wealthy) to pursue higher education."

CD loves Panamá and the people, despite horrendous experiences (Free e-book; *Fading Paradise*). He plans to spend the rest of his life in the paradise that is Panamá

- Estrelita Suarez V. de Jaramillo – 3/15/2016

CD is involved in research of natural cancer cure at this time. It has proven effective in all cases, so far. It is based on a plant that has been in use for thousands of years, is safe, available, and cheap. He has studied botany, and was cured of a serious lymphoma with use of the plant, *Ambrosia peruviana*.

Information about this cure is free on the FaceBook group, Natural medicine research. CD asks only that all who try it please report on its effectiveness on that group.

A Killer of a Detail

Prologue

Al Terns laid back on his lawn chair in what little shade the tall coconut palms provided, sipped a weak vodka Collins, and watched the boats going in and out of the canal. There seemed one hell of a lot too much traffic anymore. The local community association was going to have to put lots more pressure on the county to connect the other end of the channel to the bay so half of them could go out by the back channel.

George and Mary Banks waved to him as they went by. Al waved back.

Bill Rinks went out. Someone was with him – a woman. He always went a little too fast, causing a wake. Showing off for whatever woman he was showing off for. Al couldn't really see who she was, so didn't know if she was a local. Maybe she was that Platt girl staying with the Banks. Wouldn't she be going out with them, then?

Maybe they planned to meet on one of the many barrier islands or something.

Al was a bit of a gossip. He liked to know what was going on around him and liked to exchange stories with the women at the community center. Since Elsie died, he didn't have much else to do. Even at sixty seven he supposed he could still be dating if he'd only bother to get himself into presentable shape, but it didn't really seem worth the effort. He was never what anyone could label a "ladies man" – and he really didn't care to start now! Sex always seemed more interesting to talk about than to do, with him. He was too inhibited for today's world. His father had been a lay preacher and had drummed negativity into him until he was almost married. He hadn't ever really loved Elsie in any real romantic sense, but they'd always been good friends and had liked each other honestly and sincerely. The marriage had been a very good one. It had lasted for thirty eight years, until Elsie died of colo-rectal cancer. Their only daughter was, surprisingly, quite beautiful. They were both plain.

There came Mel Sharpe and that Lorna woman who lived with him. They'd been out in Emmet's gulf boat. They knew everybody in the neighborhood, even though they lived over by Greentree Acres Estates. Mel was the golf semi-pro at Greentree and Lorna was the tennis coach. They were a lot of fun, but Al could never quite bring himself to condone their living together. He'd renounced religion long ago, but that still smacked of sin to him.

Emmet and Sandy Klaus. Sandy Klaus, for Christ's sake! If he heard one more joke about her stupid name he'd puke! They owned a little exclusive boutique in Naples and were very popular in the neighborhood. Anybody living there was popular, for one reason or another. It was the kind of snobby exclusive place where an unpopular person could be encouraged to move elsewhere very quickly. Even that Bill Rinks fellow, as insensitive as he sometimes seemed, and a drummer for one of those rock and roll and jazz bands, was liked.

Al sighed and sipped. So he was a snob.

There went Jamie Prescott. The Platt girl waved to him from the bow of the boat, so he saluted her with his Collins. It had to be someone else on Bill's boat, so he'd been wrong on that one, but who else could it be?

Jamie owned a sports shop. Everybody in the neighborhood got all kinds of things at wholesale, so he was solidly liked.

Well, the area was filled with single women and Rinks knew most of them it seemed sometimes, so she probably wasn't anyone from the neighborhood. Musicians (if one could even call a rock drummer a musician) always seemed to attract women in droves.

Al dozed lightly off and on, waking up each time a boat would go by either way, so he saw them all come back.

Except Bill Rinks.

Bill Rinks didn't come back.

"Are you and Janet coming out to the island?" Lt. Jim Hill asked of Det. Lt. Nathaniel "Nick" Storie when Nick came into Capt. Paddy James' office.

Jim was day head of homicide and Nick was night chief. Paddy was department head.

"We plan to come out Sunday morning. We'll spend the day. She has to be back in Orlando Sunday night.

"Am I ever glad she's gonna graduate in June!"

Janet Barnes was Nick's first really serious girlfriend. He was sure he would marry her from the first time they met on a case that took him to the college she was attending. She was six years younger than him, but that didn't much matter to either of them, in any way.

"The island" was a cabin Jim built on a piece of land he'd bought on a barrier island to the south. Jim would be married in May.

The two homicide cops, Paddy, and the fourth person in the office, Sgt. Marsha Blevins, aide and secretary to Paddy (And the one who really ran the department) were close friends as well, as co-workers.

Lt. Pat Matheny, the homicide head for the graveyard shift, was quite a bit too superficial and shifty to ever become very close to anyone. He was an aspiring politician who thought and acted like any other politician.

"Chile, she's gonna *be* gradua*te*d!" Marsha corrected. "If'n you's a-gonner marry no collige girl, you's a-gonner hafta tryta learnta speak that there colligese!

"There's something odd going on at Royal Palm Estates. Somebody went out in a boat and didn't come back in. Some old guy's worried about it. Says the guy never stays out this late, or something."

"So? Have him contact the coast guard," Paddy suggested. "That's not anything to do with us, unless somebody
else *did* come back in his boat. That would raise a few
questions!"

"I already called them. The guy's the type whose hunches
are usually on the money – which he has lots of!"

"Just give it to Pat when he comes in," Jim suggested.
"He'll be impressed with almost anybody who even
possibly might donate to his campaign fund."

"Oh, lord! That's right!" Paddy said, with a sigh. "That
ass is running for the state senate, isn't he?"

"Lord, child, you is dense!" Marsha said. "He's running
for the US senate! His future pop-in-law's a *state* senator!"

"Show's what you know!" Jim replied quickly. "His
future big daddy-in-law's a state representative, not a
senator, and they wanted him for attorney general, but that
was a bit too far for him to stand a chance.

"I'll leave what's left of Friday in your capable hands.
See you on the island tomorrow, Marsh. See you on
Sunday, Nick.

"Paddy, you ought to come out to my little hideaway!
"Ciao!"

"I will *not* get into any boat! Not for *any* reason!" Paddy
replied, positively. "Have a good weekend all. I'll leave it
all to you two. Joan's got big plans for tonight, and I have
to dress up. Stupid opera or something she knows I hate.
Think it over *very* carefully before you marry that woman!
If she's better educated than you, you have to live with this
sort of thing. I *know*!"

"Paddy, you know perfectly well you love going places
with Joan. You two are inseparable and you love it!"
Marsh said, with a smirk.

"Who wouldn't?" Paddy fired back. "I only object to
which places!"

Paddy was a huge man, both in height and breadth. He could put on a brand new, expensive, tailor-made suit, and look like he'd slept in it for three nights running. His wife was a very attractive, svelte, highly educated woman. They adored one another.

Paddy and Marsha went out, teasing at each other. Nick went to his desk.

Not much happened on that shift. A man was found dead in a motel room, but it turned out to be a coronary. A woman was hit by a drunk and killed, which was, sadly, a routine matter.

When Pat came on duty at two, Nick chatted a couple of minutes, then went home for the weekend.

"Nick, do you remember that guy who went out in a boat and didn't come back in on Friday?" Marsha asked, holding her hand over the phone about half an hour into Nick's shift on Monday. She held the phone up and said, "Three."

Nick punched line three. "Yes? Nick Storie here."

"Nick? This is Sgt. Samuel Robert Keller with the Florida State Marine Patrol. You had a report that one William Cole Rinks didn't return from a boating trip into the gulf late on Friday evening?"

"Well, we didn't get any names, but yes," Nick replied, shrugging at Marsh. "Sgt. Marsha Blevins referred the report to the coast guard. I'm assuming you're talking about the Royal Palms Estates misper?"

"Affirmative. An Albert Otto Terns made the initial missing person report." Sam Keller, in those few times Nick had spoken with him, always came off sounding like Sgt. "Just the Facts M'am" Friday. He never merely said, "Al Smith" or even "Mr. Smith." It was always "Mr. Aloysias Beltheuse Smith," or something.

"You have something?"

"A twenty foot fiberglass Harborcraft boat registered to a William Cole Rinks, one forty one East Canal, was found in the mangroves on the eastern side of a small unnamed barrier island seven point five nautical miles due south of Sanibel Island. There was some blood, human, type AB negative, found on the control console, seat cushion, and decking. It appears there had been some attempts made to remove the blood. Foul play is suspected.

"Captain James Andrew Dulin suggested that you be contacted, as Mr. Albert Terns (Wonders! He left out the middle name!) primarily reported suspicion of a crime to your department. The area of residence of the possible victim of any suspected violent criminal act lies within the jurisdiction of your department, thus you are better situated to investigate certain aspects of the case."

"I see. I'll get right on it. Please give Sgt. Blevins any information you have. I'll finish this status report and go out to Royal Palms Estates immediately."

He saw Marsha listening and grinned at her. If he took the information he'd sound like Keller for an hour after.

Marsha gave him the middle finger and started taking notes.

"Mr. Al Terns? I'm Det. Lt. Nick Storie. I'd like to ask you a few questions about the report you made Friday evening," Nick said, coming into the back yard by the canal to find Terns sitting at a white wrought iron table sipping a tall vodka Collins. He'd gone to the front door to ring the bell and had heard Terns yell to come on around back.

"Had a strong hunch!" Terns greeted. "Never am wrong in my hunches!

"Elsie, she was my late wife – died, you know. Anyhow, that's all beside the point. She always said it was just plain uncanny about my hunches. Sixth sense, she said.

"When he didn't come back in time for work I knew something was wrong. Sort of added the way that woman was wrapped up and knew there was some big trouble on the horizon! You add a sexy woman to a womanizer, it's like a match to gasoline.

"Care for some Collins, Nick? Whole pitcher there. You don't have one, I'll drink it all."

"Thanks. I'd really like one, but I'm on duty at the moment. Care to connect the dots?" If Terns was going to talk in riddles he would, too.

Didn't phase him.

"Uh-huh! I do do that! Let's see.

"The Banks went out a bit before Bill and the mystery woman. They have a twenty eight foot Sea Ray. Beautiful job!

"That was about twoish. Bill and the woman went out maybe two ten or so. He always goes a bit too fast. Wake beats our stuff up, you see. Don't like it, but what can you do?

"See, I thought maybe the Platt girl was with him, but she went out about an hour later with Jamie Prescott, who owns the sporting goods store over on Davis. Gets all our sports stuff wholesale. The whole neighborhood. The Platt girl could do a lot worse. He seems a level sort. Stable, you know? Makes pretty decent money.

"Stop me when I get off the subject. I tend to babble on and on.

"Let me see, now. I remember thinking how the girl with Rinks couldn't be the Platt girl – I can never remember her first name. Penny or Betty or something such – because there she was!

"That's why I say a mystery woman. Sounds kind of mysterious.

"Mel and Lorna went out just before them in Emmet's boat. They use it a lot of the time. He's a golfer and she's tennis.

"Don't make jokes about Sandy Klaus! Please!"

"Okay," Nick said matter-of-factly. "Let's decode this.

"The Banks, who went out first? Who are they, and why did you mention them at all?"

"Because the Platt girl – Judy! Yes! That's it! – is staying with them. I wondered why she wasn't with them when they went out. That's why I thought it was probably her on Bill's boat, at first, but she went out later. With Jamie."

"They live back that way, then?" Nick pointed along the canal to the east.

"Damned county won't open up the channel-pass back there! It's already *there*! It's not like they'd have to do any major job. Maybe dig it out a few feet deeper toward the back end. It's only two hundred feet!

"Four oh three. Just this side of the bridge."

"Right. Rinks lived at one forty one, which is on the far side of the bridge. Jamie Prescott?"

"Hell of a nice guy. Lives at four fifty two, right across the street there. There's no access from that side to the canal so he keeps his boat at a private slip up just past the bridge. You saw it when you came in. Slip number's the same as his street number. Four fifty two."

"Sandy Klaus and what he has to do with it?"

"Sandy's a she. Emmet's wife. All those stupid jokes about her name near to drive me crazy! They're over in number two twelve. Other side. Keep their boat at the slips. Mel and Lorna took their boat out."

"Mel and Lorna. They're the golf and tennis people?"

"Greentree."

"You finally lost me, but I think I was doing pretty good for awhile," Nick said, with a grin.

"I like you! Got a sense of humor!" Terns poured another glass of Collins. "Mel Sharpe's the tennis pro and instructor at Greentree, and Lorna Fields is his live-in or significant other or whatever they call a shack-up nowadays.

"They went out, they came in. All of them went out, but Bill and some woman didn't come back.

"Bill's a rock and roller. Drummer. Loose women always chase musicians. I figure she was married and her husband caught them out there. She was bundled up so nobody'd know who she was, but he was following her, or something.

"Ask me, there's two bodies out there somewhere."

"There was only one type of blood in the boat. That can't tell us much, of course. We don't even know what blood type Rinks was. It could be the woman's."

"You can check the chromosomes."

"What?" Nick asked, confused again.

"X-Y cells means it's his blood."

"Oh, certainly. If Tiny gets a sample he'll check for that kind of thing right away. Can you describe the woman who was on Rinks' boat? Size? Weight?"

"Sort of brownish hair, I believe. Had on a big hat, but I could see a bit of her hair in back. Make it medium longish. Shoulder length. Wasn't fat, but she was on the deck sort of all stretched out, so I couldn't tell really. Average height or maybe a little tall. Not what you'd call petite, but I could be wrong, there. Laying sort of bent around with those mirrored sunglasses.

"She had on bright puke green stretch slacks and a loose sort of top. She had a scarf around her hair under the hat and on the sides of her face.

"That's about it. She looked familiar enough I thought it was the Platt girl, but that mainly means she was average.

"Come to think of it, now, the Platt girl's hair's more that reddish blonde, so I should have known. Didn't register 'til right now.

"Sure you won't have a short one?"

"No. I have to work until two. I'll get back if I need anything else."

"That walk-in medical clinic over on East Davis!" Terns cried, suddenly.

"What?" Nick was lost again.

"Bill had that Oriental flu bug going around so much a month or so back and thought he had encephalitis. He went to the clinic. They'll have his blood type!"

"That's certainly a help. I'll radio that in on my way on to Jamie Prescott's. He's right across the street there?"

"Yep! Drop in anytime you're around! I like to talk."

Nick saluted and headed for his car.

"Mr. Prescott, I hate to bother you like this, but we're afraid there's been foul play concerning a close neighbor." Nick apologized, after introducing himself. "Mr. Rinks went out on his boat Friday afternoon and never came back in, as you may have already heard. The Marine Patrol found his boat had drifted up among the mangroves. There's blood in it. There's no sign, either of Bill Rinks or of the unidentified woman who was seen on his boat with him early Friday afternoon.

"We've been told you were out in the gulf Friday. Did you see Rinks anywhere?"

"Yes. We saw him down to the south. It was about four, I think. I was fishing off the port side, so I saw them go by when Judy waved. I didn't pay too much attention to them, really."

"We're trying to identify the woman who was with him. We don't know if she's been reported as missing anywhere."

"She was a tall woman with a pretty good figure is all I know. She had on a two-piece sunbathing suit, not quite a bikini, but just a little more. She had on one of those big floppy straw Jamaican hats and mirrored sunglasses.

"I only saw her for a few seconds. I wasn't paying any particular attention to them and they passed off a ways to our starboard, so Judy might have seen them better."

"You say it was south?" Nick asked, writing each little detail down. He never knew what might prove important, but the fact that the woman had shed the "green stretch slacks" and "loose top" could prove very important. His list of items found in the boat didn't contain any such things. It didn't contain any items that a woman would carry more than a man – of any kind.

"It was about two miles before the ten thousand islands and maybe half a mile offshore. We were trying to catch spotted trout in the shallows. We didn't have much luck."

Nick asked a few more questions, then went out. The Banks and Judy Platt were probably his next best witnesses. It was possible Judy saw something that would identify the woman.

They weren't home, so he went to see Emmet and Sandy Klaus.

"Then you will often lend your boat to Sharpe – or anyone?" Nick asked.

"Yes. A couple of times a month," Emmet answered. "I get free golf advice and Sandy gets tennis instructions. Sandy and I went to the Medieval Pageant in Ft. Myers, so we didn't plan to use it."

"Would you care for a hot, or cold, cup of coffee,

Lieutenant?" Sandy asked. "I've got a fresh pot."

She was a comfortable, slightly plump woman in her forties, about the same age as her husband. She had mousy brown hair while Emmet only had a fringe of salt-and-pepper hair. Both wore steel rimmed glasses. Emmet, at five ten, was a couple of inches taller than Sandy.

"Lorna and Mel are popular around the area," Emmet continued. "They do favors for us and we do favors for them."

"Thank you, I would really appreciate a hot cup," Nick replied to Sandy. "Black, please," then to Emmet, "What I have to know is if they saw anything out there Friday afternoon."

"Isn't it just terrible?" Sandy said, handing Nick a large mug of very good coffee. "Bill was always a lot of fun. I just can't believe he...." she shuddered.

"He was a jazz musician," Emmet said. "He ran around with a bunch of groupies. I don't think he used drugs – except maybe marijuana sometimes – or any of that, but he couldn't keep his pants zipped.

"He started in New Orleans, which is where his first band was from. You may've heard of them, 'The Won Knight Stand?' Whole bunch were in trouble all the time. Zipper trouble, mostly. Somebody killed one of them in a brawl in a bar over some cheap whore."

"Em!" Sandy exclaimed.

"We can't be nice and follow polite conventions, Hon," Emmet pointed out. "I can see they don't believe Bill met with any accident out there.

"Lieutenant, was he murdered?"

"We don't know what happened to him. The Marine Patrol found his boat, and there was quite a lot of blood in it. It could be his or it could be the woman's who was with him or it could be a third person's. There might have been some kind of accident. He might have cut himself or any number of things, but we don't think so. We do suspect foul play, quite frankly, but we don't know if he was the victim or the perpetrator."

"Oh, boy! You really *do* use those kinds of words! " Sandy cried.

"Me? You should hear Sam Keller!" Nick grinned. "`Just the facts, M'am! Did you directly witness the alleged criminal act of jaywalking perpetrated by Mr. Alexius Peter Cadwalader Forthhampton Julianus Reginald Braithewaite the Fourth on the afternoon of August the eleventh at precisely three seventeen PM at the north corner of Fifth Avenue and Third Street in the northwest lane at which time the aforementioned individual allegedly deliberately and with malice aforethought stepped approximately four and three tenths of an inch outside of the clearly marked pedestrian lane?'"

"You're kidding!" She grinned back.

"Not much. I talked to him for about five minutes earlier today and still catch myself using that kind of language. Perpetrator *is* a word I use, though.

"Tiny, the coroner, will be doing a chromosome check to see if the blood's male or female and we're checking to see if it was Rinks' blood type. We have to know who that woman with him was."

"So. You suspect her?" Emmet asked, looking shrewdly at Nick.

"There's absolutely nothing on that boat to indicate she was ever on it. When she went out, she was wearing slacks. When they were later seen out in the gulf she was wearing a bathing suit. The slacks would logically still be in the boat unless she, or someone else, removed them, deliberately.

"Deliberately removing those items is a little detail that

shows us either she or someone else was trying to guarantee she wasn't identified as having been the one on the boat. If it was her, she did something to Rinks, and if it was someone else, she probably had something done to her. That, or she can identify whoever did whatever."

"You take on speech habits of people, don't you?" Sandy asked. "You've been talking to Al Terns."

"That obvious, huh?" He grinned.

"If you can follow him, he usually has a lot to say," Emmet said. "There's not too much that goes on around here he doesn't know about."

"He's the local village gossip, but he's never vicious with it," Sandy explained. "He drinks all day every day and talks on and on. He's never really drunk."

"He's become immune to the stuff," Emmet suggested. "I think we'd find him strange if he didn't have a few."

"He's found the formula to stay at a pleasant glow," Nick said. "The bottle only had a little bit missing and he had an almost full pitcher, so he's got it figured to about a third of a shot per glass.

"He drinks about one glass every half hour, so that's about one beer per hour in alcohol. He never really gets drunk, but his liver's on overtime if he's been doing it long."

"We've known him about nine years," Sandy agreed. "Even when Elsie was alive he was like that."

"His wife? What did she die of?"

"Female and colon cancer that spread all over," Emmet answered. "They have a daughter. Truly beautiful girl. She lives up north somewhere."

"It's really amazing how two people like Al and Elsie could have such a striking beauty for a daughter," Sandy said. "Elsie was even plainer than Al."

"I think Bill probably dated her the last time she was

here," Emmet replied. "I know Al was torn. He liked Bill, but he frowns on all pop musicians on general principles. His father was a religious fanatic, and, even though Al professes to not be religious, he still tends to judge people."

"Any specific things?" Nick asked, perking up.

"No, not really. They went out a few times," Sandy replied. "She sings. She sang for his jazz band sometimes, but lots of his girlfriends do. I think Al disapproved of the fact Rinks ever *had* all those girlfriends, more than anything else."

"Lorna Fields sang with them a few times when they played at the country club," Emmet said. "Even June."

"Well, June tried, anyhow, when they played at her place. She doesn't have much talent, I'm afraid. Lorna's pretty fair."

"June?"

"June Cerf," Sandy answered. "She owns Cerf's Surf Lounge. It's a nightclub and restaurant. She lives the next block down from here."

"Did Rinks date her?"

"Lord above, no way!" Sandy laughed. "She only dates rich old multi-millionaires! She's engaged to that Hodgkinson man who owns all that land east of Bonita and on down south. He's maybe seventy five and she's about thirty three. You can ask Al about it. He says they'd already be married if she'd agree to sign a prenuptial.

"She says she has lots of property, too, and the res-taurant. She'd be a total fool to sign any kind of agreement that would leave him everything if anything happened to her and her nothing if anything happened to him.

"He had a private detective following her once and she broke it off until he apologized and swore he wouldn't ever do that again. I suppose a seventy year old man dating a thirty year old woman has plenty to be suspicious or jealous about.

"We don't have much to gossip about around here, but what we have is juicy!

"June was supposed to go to the pageant with us, but she was called in for some emergency at the restaurant. She's really nice enough, but she's looking out strictly for number one."

"Hon, you let Al spread the gossip," Emmet cautioned. "It's mostly a bunch of hearsay. We don't *know* any of it!"

"Al Tern's never been far wrong, that I know of!" she returned, defensively. "I'm not saying anything she wouldn't admit about herself!"

Nick changed the subject. "Did Rinks ever date Lorna, or did she just sing for his band?"

"Lorna? No, she wouldn't date anyone," Sandy said. "She and Mel are too tight."

They chatted awhile, then Nick left. He drove by the Banks' to find there was still no one there.

Cerf's Surf Restaurant and Lounge, live entertainment, was only two blocks off the route back to the station, so he stopped and went in. He asked to speak with Miss June Cerf and was shown into a rather spacious and somewhat ostentatious office by the bartender, who didn't have anyone but several people working on the stage in the place. He explained the entertainment lounge was closed on Monday nights because they just had a little comedy show in the restaurant section.

Judy Cerf was a very poised, highly confident, attractive woman with reddish brown hair, startling green eyes, an exceptional figure, and a low pleasant voice. She was tall, almost six feet.

"Lt. Storie? What's the problem now? The band too loud for the bowling alley crowd?" she asked, with a dazzling smile.

"No, not that I'm aware of." Nick returned the smile. "I'm with homicide. Bill Rinks, one of your neighbors, is feared dead of foul play. We understand his band played here from time to time.

"Was there ever any kind of incident? A jealous husband or boyfriend who acted angry?"

"Bill? He doesn't have any band. He's drummer for The Gathering C, a sometimes jazz band. They've played here every two months for perhaps three years. He plays studio for rock and jazz and subs for any band who needs a really professional drummer. He's good."

"Sometimes band?"

"Jazz doesn't pay a decent living, so they booked our cycle and another club's on rotation basis. Between those two weeks every two months the guys can farm out their backup services. They're all good enough that they make plenty. The jazz is more a hobby than a business. They were supposed to play here this week, but Stinger can-celed. They got a project that pays a lot more, so they'd traded gigs with The Stranglers out there setting up now. They're to play next week, but without Bill....

"You say you think he's dead?"

Nick explained about the boat and the blood.

"I really don't see anyone wanting to kill him, unless maybe it *was* a boyfriend. It certainly wasn't any angry husband. Bill didn't do windows or married women.

"That's an inside line. We get a lot of guys like Bill, and a lot who don't care if the woman's married or not. Bill did care.

"I don't think he spent many nights alone judging by what I've seen so far."

Nick thanked her and went out front to the lounge area, where the bartender was washing glasses and watching the band put duct tape all over the stage.

"I think they use about ten rolls of that crap every time they set up," the bartender said. "All the bands do."

"Yeah. Part of the business, I guess. Have to tie down all those cords."

"Yeah, and I have to clean up after them!"

"If this section's closed Mondays, why have a bartender?"

"Restock, set up, keep an eye on the people in and out and make cocktails for the restaurant. I'm Len, by the way.

"What're we in for today? Complaints about the noise, or the church bitching because we sell demon rum at all?"

"No. I'm working on a murder case." A bored waitress came in a side door to hand Len a slip of paper. He dropped four glasses onto her tray and quickly made two perfect Manhattans and two Old Fashioneds, punched on the cash register, took the money from a twenty she handed him, and dropped the change on her tray.

"They pay the bar separately," Len said, coming back to sit a cup of coffee in front of Nick. He poured one himself. "Stinking system. I don't get any tips, but June pays extra for Monday.

"You got a few minutes to talk? I go bugs out here.

"What's this place got to do with any murder?"

"It's not definite there's been any murder, but we think Bill Rinks is dead. We found his boat and a lot of blood. He never came home. Miss Cerf's a neighbor, and he played in a band here. We needed to know if anyone saw or heard anything to give us a direction. Bill was quite the man for the ladies, or so I've heard."

"Bill? Aw, no! Bill's a nice guy! Really?

"He was what you call discriminating, with the women. They liked him because he was so sensitive – and it didn't hurt he looked like that tennis pro guy, Agassi! He treated all of them like he respected them. They eat that stuff up.

"I'm sorry to hear that. I hope like hell you're wrong.

"Some guy in a band he was with in New Orleans was murdered. That happened right in the middle of June's Place.

"They were supposed to play here this week."

"So Miss Cerf informs me. They canceled, and she had to come in Friday afternoon to book these guys?

"June's Place?"

"I guess she came in for that, too. She came in for something – in a hell of a lousy mood. I sort of wondered why they traded gigs. Barney, he's sax man and leader of the Stranglers – the fat one – said they traded bookings on Thursday so Stinger – the keyboard man with The Gathering C – called him up late and said they were booked for a prob three straight at New Jazz Gems.

"Miss Cerf had a cheap little club out towards the lake in New Orleans. She inherited it. It was one of those mixed rough beer and wine taverns, but she got enough for it to get out and move down here. The clientele were the kinds who brawled a lot."

"I don't understand a lot of those musician's terms. What does that stuff about the band mean?"

"Three straight's three straight days booked and New Jazz Gems is a studio," Len answered, looking around and pouring a dash of Kahlua into his own and Nick's coffee, then slipping the bottle back under the counter. "June'd raise hell if she knew I did that, okay?"

Nick grinned and nodded.

"Anyhow. New Jazz Gems is a local recording studio. Some big blow's in town and wants to jam cut a couple spontaneous. The Gathering's known all over for their jam work, so they'd make a sixer or eighter. They'll do that sometimes. We just swing our cycle.

"Now I'll translate.

"A local recording studio called The Gathering C and offered them six or eight times what they'd make here in a week to play jam improv behind a big known star for three nights. Stinger called and June booked The Stranglers in their place, so they'd play The Stranglers' gig here next month."

"Happen much?"

"Sometimes. Maybe once a year or so. It's part of the business."

"So then Miss Cerf had to change her plans for Friday. That would be why she didn't go to Ft. Myers with Sandy and Emmet Klaus. She had to be here."

"Yeah, I guess. She gets in that office and sorta camps sometimes. You were in there, so you know it's a lot like a luxury condo."

"Hah! If I had a place like that to stay I'd never go home!"

"Me neither. She even stays in there sometimes overnight ... when business is ... I should learn when to keep my mouth shut! "

"I hear her ancient lover even has a private detective checking on her. You didn't hear me say that, either!

"I suppose she would try to find some entertainment on the side, now and then. I can't see any seventy year old handling a woman like that. I can't see many guys *my* age handling it!"

"She's discreet, you know." He said with a relieved grin. "Sometimes, when the pressure's building up too much, she has a long late night business conference with somebody. She's usually pure hell on wheels for a couple days afterward. Scared we'll blab, or something.

"When something's not going right she locks herself inside that office. We know better than to bother her."

"She could lock the office and sneak out back," Nick suggested, thoughtfully. "Her boyfriend's private detective would never know she was gone. Neither would you."

"Oh, we'd know all right!" he argued, and went to take an order from another waitress. He made six drinks, made the change and came back.

"How would you know? All you'd know is she went in and locked the door."

"When she's in that kind of bad mood she uses the inside phone to bitch about everything all the time." He grinned. "It's not like she does it much, but when something goes wrong. We wait her out and she apologizes when she gets over it."

"So you know for a fact she was in there Friday. That gives her an alibi, if she needs one."

"Friday she fired Connie, then hired her back – Connie's the cute redheaded waitress that came in right after you stopped. She called me and said it was my ass if she saw spots on the glasses that night. She called later to say I'd screwed up the mix order and she'd have to spend the whole damned day trying to keep the damned business out of bankruptcy. She called about eight to apologize about that because she read a two-case order as a twenty-case order or something such.

"She was in there, alright, and a lot worse than usual! The inside phones were sizzling for awhile!"

Two waitresses came in at once. Nick thanked him, tossed down the coffee, and left.

Greentree was out on the Trail East. It wasn't too far, so Nick went right instead of left out of the restaurant. He'd take a chance Mel Sharpe and Lorna Fields would be there. He might as well get all the background done, in case he even had a case. A radio check showed it was a quiet night at the station, but that was normal since the tourist season was over.

The country club was one of those overdone things so common in the area. Janet would cringe and call it "Tourist Tacky" from something she'd read by John D. MacDonald. It did look like a cheap imitation of a cheap imitation to Nick.

Mel wasn't around, but Lorna was on the back courts, so he watched her play and instruct for twenty minutes, then went to ask if he could have just a few minutes.

"Sure! I'm all done for tonight!" she replied. "Come on into my office, okay? I have to get out of these things."

He followed her into a nice office, where she took off her shoes and socks and went into a frosted glass door to a shower.

"Sandy called me and told me about Bill," she said, tossing her shorts and shirt over the door. They were followed by the undergarments and the sound of the shower.

"I have to learn everything anyone knows while it's fresh. We don't know for certain we have a case, but I think we do. Al Terns said you and Mel were out in Emmet's boat, so you might have seen them out there somewhere.

"Did you?"

"We passed them at the outer channel marker. They turned south and we went on out."

"What can you tell me about the woman with him?"

"She was laying on the bow decking in green tights and a big floppy Jamaican straw hat." She turned off the shower. "She was talking on the phone. Bill waved and we waved back. I didn't pay too much attention to her. Mel probably didn't even see her from down there. He was inside and I was up on the cabin. He doesn't like to drive from the flying bridge when it's choppy like that.

"Do you play tennis?"

"Noy much. No golf either. I like swimming and scuba diving and volleyball. Water skiing's fun."

"Beach and water. You've got a pretty good build for tennis and basketball. You're quick.

"Which one of us knocked Bill off?"

Nick grinned as she stepped out of the shower stall with a towel partly covering her. "Oh, that! We believe Mel killed him in a fit of jealous rage because of your affair with him."

"In my wildest dreams!" she answered, with an impish leer. "He was really a dream stud. Looked like Andy A, so any tennis broad would naturally flip. Trouble was, *Bill* wouldn't play those idiotic games, because he considered me and Mel as a couple. If I would've made it with him, Mel would just consider it a license for him to make it with some other broad. We're pretty realistic about that sort of thing – which is why I'd flirt and tease, but never actually do anything. Mel wouldn't either.

"I might've with Bill. I think he'd be worth it."

"You say the woman was talking on a phone? On the boat?"

"Oh, sure! Lots of people take their cellulars out or use SS." She slipped a dress over her head, letting the towel drop at the same time. Nick looked away, which amused her. "I call on the SS on Sandy's boat all the time."

"I see. You only saw them that once?"

"Uh-huh. We went on out and did some grouper fishing off the six mile reef. We're having the catch for supper. Mel's cooking it now. Care to join us?"

"I'm on duty. I have to get back. Thanks."

"Learn anything?" Pat Matheny asked as he checked in as Nick checked out. "I hear you have a little case to fill the dreary hours."

"I might have a case. I think I have. So far, I have nothing. Not even a vague suspect, but then, I don't have a body or anything, either."

"Tiny left a note here for you," Pat said. "It's there on my desk. Par for the course."

Nick took the note. The blood in the boat was male and the clinic confirmed it was Rinks' type. That was exactly what Nick expected.

"I called you to come in early today because you now have a case," Paddy said Tuesday morning about ten in his office. "You always do work days when you have something. I know you've already put a lot of the background together. I read your files.

"Marsha, you took that report. You tell Nick about it, then we can have a little conference."

"The deceased body of one William Cole Rinks was discovered at approximately eight fifteen this morning tangled among the roots of red mangroves in the mouth of Parson's Creek where it meets Otter Run Bay four tenths of a mile south by southeast of Kimmins Point, at which the fiberglass Harborcra...." Marsha began.

"Knock it off!" Nick demanded. "So Sam Keller called you to say they found Rinks' body."

She grinned at Nick, and continued, "He'd been shot once in the back and once in the upper left side with a twenty five automatic. The second one killed him.

"That's about what a report almost twelve minutes long actually said.

"I vote we let Paddy take the next call from Keller!"

"Yeah, right," Paddy replied, as Jim came in. "Jim, you've read Nick's report on Rinks. Any suggestions?"

"Can Terns prove he was there in that lawn chair from about three o'clock, when the last boat he mentioned went out, and five thirty, when the first of them came back in? Was he really upset far more than he let on about Rinks dating his daughter? Does he even realize that Rinks, if he dated her, slept with her as well, and how does he react?"

"I have to check on that," Nick said. "Can Mel and Lorna prove they went on out and that they didn't follow Rinks?

Did Rinks ever actually make it with Lorna?"

"And can Jamie Prescott and Judy Platt prove they didn't follow them?" Marsha asked. "Did Rinks make it with Judy, who Prescott considers his own girl?"

"You'll still have to interview the Banks and Miss Platt," Paddy pointed out. "What about them? Was Rinks messing with Miss Platt? Did they disapprove?"

"Is there any way the Cerf woman can prove she was actually in her office?" Jim asked. "Was he ever one of her special `business conferences' the bartender mentioned?"

"If they don't find a woman's body, who was the woman on his boat?" Marsha asked. "Did some other musician have any reason to want to get rid of Rinks?"

"How many boyfriends did Rinks get in bad with through his womanizing?" Nick asked. "I think I have enough background to keep busy on today. First off, I have to see Judy Platt and the Banks. Maybe that alone will eliminate some of them."

"Do you have any hunches?" Jim asked.

"Just a couple of maybe's," Nick answered. "They're pretty weak, but it's something I can check, I think.

"You noticed the woman was using a phone out there?"

"Oh, yeah! If it was ship to shore the phone company should have records," Marsha said.

"If it was cellular and was one of your suspects they'll also be in the carrier records," Paddy pointed out. "You should be able to trace that, at least."

"If it was boosted cellular, the calls will be reported from the nearest pickup, probably on an island like where my place is," Jim suggested.

"If any of them have a cellular phone I can locate time and duration of the calls and the nearest pickup tower," Nick agreed. "That'll put it right smack dab in someone's lap!

"If it's not one of my suspects, I'm in trouble. I can check on all calls from the general area."

"Interview that Platt woman and the Banks, first," Paddy said. "Jim, there's a domestic abuse thing out the trail you'll have to investigate. It got messy to the degree it might turn into M one.

"Marsha, get Commissioner Morgen on the phone for me, then I'll contact Judge Collins and get a court order for you to see the records of the phone company, Nick. It'll be on your desk later.

"Well? Get cracking! You're not among the most highly paid government employees in the entire state to be standing around this office!"

Nick and Jim saluted him with their middle fingers, grinned, and went out. Nick sat at his desk to read the report on Rinks, then headed for the Banks home.

"I'm glad I finally caught you," Nick said to Mary Banks. "I have to ask you a few questions about Friday afternoon.

"Is your husband or Miss Judy Platt around?"

"They went out fishing, but they'll be back in a half hour. We're going to the new boat show this afternoon. In Ft. Meyers.

"Is it about poor Bill Rinks? Have they learned anything yet?"

"Yes, I'm afraid so. The MP found his body this morning, not far from where they found his boat. He was most definitely murdered.

"According to Al Terns you went out about the same time Rinks did. Did you see him anywhere?"

"Well, no, not that I recall. We just went out the channel and north to New Pass, where we met the Ed Gardeners and shared a picnic. They live over in Bonita Springs and have use of the island. We had the picnic and visited until around a quarter to five, then we came back in.

"Those people using the Klaus' boat were a little ahead of us. They came in from the reef and showed us two grouper they caught."

"Did Miss Platt mention having seen Rinks out there to you?"

"Oh, yes! When we heard he was missing she said he was out south with some girl. She said they went by no more than a hundred feet away and the girl seemed angry about something. She was yelling into a phone.

"She wasn't yelling at Bill. She was mad at someone on the phone. Judy didn't hear much, but she said it sounded like she was really telling off a boyfriend or something."

"I see. Miss Platt didn't recognize the woman?"

"She said she was tall, but she had on a big hat and a scarf around her face and was wearing gloves."

"Gloves?! And that didn't make Miss Platt suspicious?"

"Suspicious? Why, no. Why would it?" she asked, looking at him strangely.

"But why would anyone in a bathing suit wear gloves?"

"She had light skin. She wanted to protect it from the sun. A lot of women cover their face and hands in the sun. The skin ages very fast from sun damage on the face, particularly, and on the hands. The rest of the body doesn't show it nearly so much. I wear gloves if I'm going to be out for long. I also wear a wide hat and sunglasses in the sun. Women have been wearing gloves and big hats for centuries for that same reason. That's why women gardeners are always depicted in hats and gloves, as well as all the women on those safaris and old western things."

"I never thought of that point, but you're right!" Nick exclaimed. "I've never once wondered why ... I thought the gloves were to keep dirt off, but the pictures always showed the women picking flowers or herbs. I'll be damned! My own girlfriend wore gloves when we went fishing on Sunday. I never thought about it.

"I'll be damned! You live and learn!"

"Men aren't very observant of women's hands. They tend to look at legs and bosoms.

"I hear the boat coming in. George always honks three short blasts to tell me I can get the lunch on the table. You can ask Judy about seeing them, but break it to her about them finding Bill's body as easily as you can. She was a little sweet on him."

Nick nodded and went to the dock down by the bridge, where Judy Platt was standing on the dock, looping the bow line around a tie-down peg. She looked up and smiled. Nick couldn't help noticing she was more than average good looking.

"Miss Platt? I'm Lt. Nick Storie. May I ask you a few questions?"

"About Bill? Have they found him?"

"I'm afraid so."

"Oh, no! If you say it that way ... he's dead?" she asked, shock evident on her face. "Give me a minute? I expected it, but I did hope...."

"I'm sorry. Everyone seems to have liked him. I'll ask Mr. Banks a couple of questions first."

"You will? What's going on?" George asked, coming from the stern line.

"I'm Det. Lt. Nick Storie from Naples South Station, Homicide," Nick introduced, offering his hand. "I'm here investigating the murder of Bill Rinks.

"I've spoken with your wife and she didn't remember seeing Mr. Rinks Friday. Did you?"

"No. We went on up north to New Pass. Judy saw him, though. Some woman was with him.

"So he was murdered? You know that for sure?"

"I'm afraid so. His body was found earlier this morning. We're trying to find who the woman was who was out there in that boat with him."

"Hmm. Could'a been almost anybody. He didn't stick with any one more than a day. Beats me why they didn't seem to care!"

"Oh, Uncle George!" Judy said. "Bill never pretended he was in love or even interested in anything steady. We dated several times, not only once.

"Mr. Storie, he didn't mark up his conquests on some kind of conquest list or other, he only dated women he could respect. He was interested in people as people and he'd do anything he could to help anybody who needed him. He was somebody anyone could just *talk* with about absolutely anything. He really understood. It wasn't an act. We didn't compete for him – because it wouldn't do any good, and we knew it."

"I'm beginning to see. I'm not beginning to understand it, yet, but I don't understand my own fiancee, so I surely couldn't understand anyone else.

"Mrs. Banks said you told her that the woman seemed to be having an argument with someone on the phone?"

"It sounded like it. She was yelling about something, but I couldn't hear any of the words. Our motor was too loud. It was more the way she was waving her arm around and the tone that made me think probably she was having a fight with a boyfrien.... Oh! Dear God! She might have been telling some lunatic boyfriend she was out there with Bill! Oh, my God!"

"We'll have to find out everything we can about that one. Can you describe her?"

"I couldn't see anything except for her shape. She was tall and very, what you'd call statuesque. Fair skin."

"Well, every little bit helps. If you can think of anything

else at all, call me, please?" He gave her a card. She nodded.

"I suppose I'll call on Terns again while I'm out here."

"If anyone knows anything, he's it!" George agreed. "Not much gets past him."

"He said he saw you go out and come in." Nick grinned. "He saw everyone go out and come in – except Bill didn't come in, so he called in the missing persons report that got us into it early.

"Do either of you know definitely the names of any girls Bill was dating?"

"Cetainly. There was Amy Fletcher," Judy answered. "She was more serious than he liked, but they'd worked it out, I'm sure. She lives in Parkwood Dream Condos, but I don't know which one."

"OK. I'll find her. I guess I'll stop by at Al's first."

"Al's really sweet," Judy said. "Tell him hello for me."

Nick chatted a minute, then headed for Al's.

"Ah! Still on duty?" Al greeted. "If not, pour yourself a tall one! They're not too strong.

"Hear they found Rinks. Shot full of holes. (Damn it! Now I can't use the old, `Ahha! And how did *you* know he was shot, huh!?' routine, Nick thought.) Haven't found the woman.

"There'll be bunch of women who'll cry over him, I suppose.

"Know who the woman was yet?"

"Not even maybe perhaps. I've been thinking about some things you might be able to help with, assuming you didn't go out there and plug him yourself."

"Me? Why would I do that? I'm very flattered you think I'd have the nerve to shoot somebody – I think – but why me?"

"Why not? I have to suspect everyone in the state I wasn't with the whole afternoon on Friday. He'd dated your daughter, and you certainly would never approve of that. No father would."

"He probably slept with her, far as that goes. A father wants his daughter to be pure until she gets married. I've asked a couple of girls I know have slept with him why they didn't seem to get pissed because he slept with everybody. They all said it wasn't that way with Bill.

"What the hell is that supposed to mean? In my day, a woman only slept with a man after she was guaranteed they'd get married! Now they sleep with some Bill Rinks because he's so understanding and sweet? Excuse my ass if that's 'way too modern for me! Damned pill was the worst thing ever happened to this world! Girls asked *him* to bed them! They figured he was doing *them* the favor!

"I waved to everybody who went in or out, so I was here. Doc and Frannie were pan fishing over on their dock next door all afternoon. We hollered at each other every once in awhile. Doc came over for a drink, once. No way I could've gone out. My boat never left the dock last Friday. That's another thing.

"Don't have any idea who she was?"

"The woman, seen by umpty dozen people on the boat, but who nobody, so far, can describe, beyond that she's tall and has a good figure? No. We know very little about that one.

"Know any names you can give me of the girls who slept with him, then didn't care that he slept around?"

"She shot him full of holes. She went out all wrapped up so nobody'd know who she was. She'd planned to shoot him all along. There has to be some big reason for that."

"She wasn't still on the boat and she didn't leave so much as a single fingerprint on it," Nick agreed. "That means she had to have gotten off of it sometime after Miss Platt and Mr. Prescott saw him.

"Did someone meet her out there or did she go to land – and how? I should be asking Judy and Jamie who else they saw down there.

"There has to be a motive, too. I'll have to dig for that. I'll have to check several things I have already."

"Hmm, Well there was Rita Gomez, sort of fiery type, and has a way to look that makes you wonder if she's as hot as her eyes, if you get the drift. She claimed she wouldn't be bothered if he slept around because a woman would have to expect that in such a man.,Her and a Kitty Something-or-other both told me the very same thing. It sort of shocked me at the time, but that's the way they live today."

"Do you know where those two girls live?"

"Rita lives over the canal in that pink stucco house. He topped off his glass. "Kitty's from New Jersey and went back up about three months ago. Couldn't find work here."

"I'll have to call on Rita Gomez, I suppose."

"You have an idea who did it, don't you?" Al asked, giving Nick the shrewd look again. "Some woman."

"Within a few possibilities, I think just maybe I do. It's a matter of tying up loose details. The killer made some pretty stupid mistakes – or else the killer's deliberately leaving trails that lead nowhere.

"This one's a puzzle. I can't find the damned motive."

"Unless someone's lying."

"The trouble with that comes down to nobody lying or most of them lying. I can't see any motive for the ones I think might have done it."

"You have a good idea who it was."

"I know who I personally *think* did it, but I don't dare concentrate on that one because it's too easy to be wrong.

If I waste a lot of my time on the wrong suspect I'll lose the real killer."

"The only thing I can suggest is to have another drink!" Al happily poured one for himself.

"So! How can I get in touch with your daughter?" Nick asked. He was somewhat surprised when Al grinned broadly and gave him the address and phone number.

"Miss Platt, I have to check on one more thing while I'm out here. I have to know if you recognised anyone else from around here immediately before or anytime after you saw Rinks down by the Ten Thousand Islands?"

"Please call me Judy," she answered, thinking deeply. "Let me try to picture it. There were four or five other boats in the area, but none of them seemed familiar, in any particular way. One was a big blue and white cabin job, two of ... no, three ... were eighteen or twenty footers. Those walkthroughs, like Jamie's. Not the cabin.... There were two boats, little Johnboats, on the pieces of shell beach. I saw them through the binoculars. Two families were having a picnic. Two men, two women and three children. I saw a small aluminum boat, maybe a twelve footer, with one of those little ten or fifteen horse outboards on it anchored just inside the bay. `Diver down' flags around it, so people would give it a good wide berth in that shallow water. The divers couldn't go deep enough to avoid your prop.

"No. I'm afraid there was no one from around here but Jamie and me and Bill and that woman. There were several commercial fishermen. Two boats, I think. They're always out around those shallows."

"What? Crabbers? Gillnetters?"

"Gillnetters. Mullet fishermen. One in a green boat with one of those lights on a boom and one white boat with the console in the middle. One of those things that look like they're rearing out of the water in front."

"What are you looking for?" George Banks asked. "You thought of something or Al said something for you to come back."

"The woman has never been found, so either her body's somewhere out there or someone took her off Bill's boat. Add to that, the killer, if it wasn't the woman, had to get out there, somehow."

"Why does it have to be someone from right around here?" Mary Banks asked.

"It doesn't, but ninety five percent of the murders I've investigated were committed by someone familiar with the victim, usually family or close friend. This kind of murder demands a solid motive. It wasn't some random violence thing."

"I don't know," Mary said. "You read in the papers all the time about maniacs. Somebody could have killed Bill and raped the woman with him."

"Those kinds of murders usually come in a definite series. The woman had a phone, so she would have called nine one one or something as soon as they were attacked, even if she knew the attacker.

"I'm wondering about that cell phone! Would whoever she was talking to hear the boat?"

"But! That means she killed Bill! There's no other...!" Judy cried.

"The cell phones have a damper on the mouthpiece. They don't pick up traffic noises," George said. "I guess she did have to be the killer, didn't she?"

"It's more than fifty-fifty." Nick asked a few more questions, then headed for the next street and Rita Gomez. She wasn't home today, but a maid at told him she was at the community center, so he headed there.

"Miss Gomez, I have a few questions. It's about Bill Rinks," Nick said, after introducing himself.

Rita was tall and attractive, with an exceptional figure and long dark auburn hair. Nick could see what Al meant about her eyes.

"I cried myself to sleep about Bill," she replied. "He was a wonderful man. I wanted more than anything in life to be the special one to him."

"He wasn't the kind to be faithful to one woman," Nick replied, watching her carefully.

"Verdad. It would not be fair for any woman to ask that he be a one woman man. Bill, he was, how you say?, the dream of a man. He had such fire and passion, but he was so, so ... honest. It mattered true to him about me, about the others. We were not only just another woman he used and threw away. He cared."

"For all of you?"

"Si. It is so sad there is no other man in the whole world who is like he was." Tears started at the corners of her eyes. "He could love truly all he loved, but he could never be in love. Do you understand?"

"No. I've never known anyone like he seems to have been.

"You were in love with him?"

"Oh, si! Es cierto! We all were in love with him."

"You understand that I have to ask you where you were last Friday afternoon and evening?"

"I was here, at home, shopping, at the beach – who knows? I was everywhere. I could kill myself for Bill, but I could never kill him!"

"That seems to be the general consensus," Nick replied, dryly. "Somebody *did* kill him."

"Sorry to bother you, but I have to ask you a question or

two," Nick said, looking around J. T. Prescott's Sportsman Supplies. "It's about the Rinks murder.

"Did you see anyone down in the Ten Thousand Islands area who was familiar, in any way – other than Rinks?"

"Just Ted and Carla ... no, that was way north when we were on the way in," Jamie replied. "Not that I can recall.

"Lieutenant, have you checked with the phone company? That woman was using a phone, so there's SS or boosted cellular. Bill didn't have either on his boat, so it'll be in the woman's name – and there are records."

"Oh? Did you make any calls from out in the gulf?"

He got a grin back. "CB. No phone or SS."

"There are a lot of CB messages back and forth. She was using a phone. That could be a stroke of luck."

"It's funny, but I just can't picture any woman killing Bill. They never even got jealous because he slept around. It's too bad you didn't know him. As much as I tried, I simply couldn't find a reason to dislike him."

"Much as you tried?"

"Hell, man! Women were always coming onto *him* for bedtime sports! I work like all hell and don't get very much! I compose the perfect line to drop in at the perfect time, and they laugh in my face! He acted a little interested and they fell all over him.

"The women weren't jealous, but I was! I tried my best to get pissed about it, but it didn't work.

"What it boils down to is he was very much the type I wished I could be. I've tried to get Rita Gomez to even look at me. She doesn't know I exist.

"Rita's a real beauty who's staying across the canal. She hops right over to Bill's place anytime he snaps his fingers for her. Judy goes around with me a bit, but I know damned well he could have said one word and she'd drop me.

"The trouble is, for me to get PO'ed, he'd have to actually do something like that. I know damned well he never would."

"I've seldom come across anyone both men and women liked so consistently. Is it `Don't speak ill of the dead' or is it real?"

"I never knew anyone quite like him, either. It *is* real, at least in my case. He had a sort of balance of some kind where he was one of the guys and some kind of dream stud to the women. Bottle whatever it was and you could soon pay off the national debt with leftover pocket change."

"Well, I have to get my court order and see who called whom out there," Nick said, sighing deeply. "`Neither man nor woman would so despoil, Would ever bend or stoop, To take the nurture from this soil, E'er would kill Lord Proute.'"

"Say what?" Jamie asked, giving Nick a wary look.

"It's a quote from an English poem that seems to me more than apropos. It fits, somehow."

"Miss Amy Fletcher? I'm investigating the killing of William Rinks," Nick said, after she answered the carved mahogany door, glanced at the badge in his hand, looked him up and down and said, "Come in," in a low, husky, voice. She was tall and statuesque, with long dark hair. Bill seemed to like that type. Amy Fletcher was a knock-out, and knew it.

"God, that was a shock!" she cried. "I mean, nobody would ever want to hurt Bill. He was just, well, like a combination guy."

"Combination guy?"

"Sort of like a close brother, on one level. You could confide in him and know it stopped right there. You could tell him anything. He'd really try to help anyone who came to him. He was also the greatest thing to happen to the American bedroom since seventeen seventy six!

"It wasn't so much that he had such a great technique, it was more that you knew he wasn't simply using you. He took time to find out about you.

"Actually, his technique was nothing to sneer at, either – Why, lieutenant! You're blushing! How refreshing!"

"Uh, you were in love with him?" Nick asked, feeling the heat in his face.

"Certainly I was in love with him! Who wasn't who ever met him? So?"

"It didn't bother you that he slept with every other woman in town?"

"He slept with a few of us he could relate to, who he could respect, and who he could love. The only drawback was that he couldn't be IN love with any of us."

"I see. Another woman used almost exactly those same words about him an hour ago. Where were you last Friday afternoon?"

"Here, mostly." She flashed a small amused smirk. "I don't have a hint of an alibi.

"Bill Rinks was far too valuable a human being for anyone to kill."

"As I replied very recently to that very same suggestion, we have to face the fact that somebody did. Can you give me any names of others he was dating regularly?"

"Bill didn't date us, lieutenant, he slept with us and cared about us.

"You're blushing again.

"Rita Gomez, Eileen Riordan, Kitty Liston, Judy Platt. I don't know how many others. Eileen and Kitty weren't around for awhile."

"I've heard of all those. Thanks."

"If that takes care of the business end, shall we see if you blush all over?" she said, grinning at him.

"Unlike the late Bill Rinks, I stick with one at the time," Nick replied, with an attempt to match the grin.

"Oh? Do I denote disapproval?" She archedg her left eyebrow.

"Strangely, no. Maybe a little jealousy."

"Well, come back to see me whenever you're in the market. I'm right here, most of the time. You don't need an appointment."

"I don't think so."

"I knew you wouldn't. I'm having some fun with you, Nick. I don't sleep around. Just with Bill, and I don't have him anymore. You're a very attractive man. I might get serious about your type, and I'm not ready for that gig, yet.

"I hope you find whoever killed Bill. I want to see them fry! Slowly. *That*, lieutenant, is not in fun!"

"Learned anything new?" Jim asked, when Nick went into the station office. "You can tell me over lunch."

Nick read the messages on his desk, put the court order in his pocket, and went with Jim and Marsha to lunch at a little Italian restaurant a few blocks away. They discussed the case, but could only decide the woman had to be either the killer or the killer's accomplice.

"She had an accomplice, that's sure!" Marsha said.

"How do you figure?" Jim asked.

"The boat stayed out there while, she didn't," Marsha replied. "She didn't walk any seven miles through mangrove swamps back."

"That's something I'll have to check, after I've finished checking the phone company," Nick agreed. "Where was the closest place she could have gone to land down there? Could the boat have drifted to where it was ... that doesn't make any sense. The boat wouldn't drift back to that close to the body. We're left with an accomplice. Period."

"It really does look that way," Jim agreed. "Like you say, she didn't walk that seven miles or more back, and nobody followed them out there. Platt and Prescott would have noticed, even if it was quite a bit later. Have you considered that?"

"Uh-huh. I think he was directed to that particular spot, somehow."

"Maybe with ship to ship rather than ship to shore?" Marsha asked. "There'd still be records."

"It still doesn't make sense, because all the larger boats carry CBs to talk back and forth on. The thing is, anyone could listen, so she'd have to use the phone if she wanted to ... suddenly I'm very curious about something!"

"What might that be?" Jim asked.

"Can I take your boat down there in the morning, Jim? I want to check on something. There is one major item that's very much out of place in what Judy Platt saw."

Jim shrugged, took out his key ring, slid off the key to his boat and flipped it to Nick. He raised an eyebrow, but didn't ask what Nick was thinking.

"I'll go out tomorrow," Nick said. "Early. I want to check with the MP for the exact location – which probably means I have to listen to Florida Marine Patrol Sergeant Samuel Robert Keller. Damn!

"I have to know the exact location of some things."

"I have his report," Marsha suggested, dryly. "Maybe the loran numbers would help? Maybe the copy of the marked charts he sent us? Maybe pages and pages of very minutely detailed descriptions of the tree crabs, birds, dead fish, live fish, palm trees, shells, beer cans, seaweed and mangroves? Or maybe the angle of the sunlight through the branches over the boat? Maybe the strange kind of knot in the anchor rope?"

"I love you!" Nick cried. "The loran numbers and the charts will do.

"Strange knot in the anchor rope?"

"Yeah. Apparently a sheepshank with a fisherman's knot looped around a piece of wood, apparently builder's grade pine, two inch by two inch sawed to a length of six and one quarter inches. The one-half inch diameter bright yellow polypropylene rope was coiled under the bow on the equipment shelf that extended three quarters of the way from the point of the bow back toward...."

"Jeez! I get the idea," Jim said. "He carried a piece of wood to put in a loop to shorten the anchor rope."

"Hey, Honky! I had to write up three miserable damned pages about that stupid damned knot!" Marsha cried. "It was something standard?!"

"Sure! If you anchor in both front and back to hold you in a fishing spot you want the lines fairly tight to keep you from swinging, so you use various loop knots to shorten the rope, then pull the final loop around something. You release the whole mess by pulling out the pin or piece of wood or PVC or whatever," Jim explained. "About a third of the boats out there have something like that, if they fish the shallows."

"Crap! He thought it might have some significance, like in a satanic ritual!" Marsha cried, then started giggling. They all three got the giggles. Paddy came in to find them in a very silly mood.

"I have a court order to locate and search records of calls on ship to shore, ship to ship, or cellular, to and from this area" Nick explained to Frances Anne Parker, Supervisor and PR (And everything else. It was only a relay station) for the phone company's South Offices Station near

Everglades City. It was the closest cell and SS boost relay to the Ten Thousand Islands and Chokaloskee.

"The SS things are easy to trace, but cellular? You have to check those types of calls with the individual carriers. There are two operating down here," Frances explained. "They have towers we share on a leasing agreement with them because it would be too expensive for each company to build a tower."

"They're billed through you?" Nick asked. She just looked at him.

"This is a murder investigation." He decided to embellish, trying to get a little help. "There could be a serial killer out there. We have to trace a clue while it's fresh to save no-one-knows how many lives!"

"Oh, my dear me! What kind of serial killer? Oh, dear me!" She was almost drooling. Nick knew he had her.

"Well, this must stop right here, is that clear? We *must not* allow the killer to know we have any way to possibly track him down!"

"Oh, dear me! What's happened?"

"Well, a Naples man, Bill Rinks, went out into the gulf with a girlfriend last Friday – that's the latest victim that we know of. They found his body. He was shot. More than once. They found his boat covered with blood. Lots of violence.

"*But*! The girlfriend was *not* found! No trace of her!

"Now, there's one theory – you didn't hear this story from me. We can't stand any panic – one theory I've heard is that there's some maniac who killed Rinks and abducted the woman, possibly to hold her captive somewhere and repeatedly rape her, then to also kill her when he's had ... what he wants!

"It sounds like some cheap tabloid story I know, but that theory was expressed to me directly!"

"Oh, dear! I read about Mr. Rinks in the paper! It was out by the islands! My husband and I go out there all the time for blue crabs! Oh, dear! It's all so terribly *frightening*!

"I can access the computer billing records. Would that help?"

"Certainly! Mrs. Parker, you might possibly save who knows how many innocent peoples' lives with your prompt cooperation!" Nick blubbered back, as she steered him into a small office that had a computer terminal and a dot matrix printer, along with a few file cabinets.

An hour later he had a list of names, times and billing numbers. He thanked Mrs. Parker and again swore her to total silence.

He took the lists back to the office, locked them in his desk, took the charts Marsha gave him out to Prescott's, then to the Banks (Who were just getting home from the boat show) to have the exact locations of everything marked, went to supper, then reported for his night shift duty.

Paddy had put Ed Goins on homicide detail night shift until further notice, so Nick poured over the lists for three hours. Nothing.

He listed everything suspicious and put the lists back into his desk. If he thought of anything else he'd want them where he could reach them quickly.

He went home to bed. In the morning he was going for a boat ride.

There were some banks of offshore fog early that quickly burned off to leave a brilliant day with a light easterly wind. The tide was high, so Nick could stay out enough to make good time. He went to the loran position where the Rinks boat was found and sighted back. He saw several long islands and hundreds of smaller odd-shaped ones peppered across the field of view.

He went slowly back northward and out into the gulf to sit about where Judy had marked they'd been on the chart. The tiny island with a thin beach of ground oyster shell on the gulfward side was easy to find from there. He went in to draw the boat onto the little fan-shaped spit and look around, picking up some beer and soda cans and some paper cartons to throw into Jim's garbage sack. What he was looking for was on the northern end of that long island nearby.

He idled the boat along and around, finding there was no wash channel there at all. It was grass flats and only five feet deep at almost high tide. As he had suspected. No one was scuba diving there at half tide on Friday. Someone put that boat at that spot, anchored it securely, and put "diver down" flags around to keep anyone from approaching closely. The killer didn't need an accomplice. She had a boat waiting right there all the time to take in to shore.

He didn't really need to prove that, only to be able to show it as likely, but his luck was holding, so he'd see if he could find anyone who'd seen the boat being placed or who had seen it earlier.

Nick used his binoculars to view the nearby area. There were several smaller boats out in the flats, but they wouldn't be too likely to have been around Friday. He saw another little beach eastward on a small island, so went over to inspect it on the theory the killer could probably lure Rinks to a particular spot easily, then the killer could almost walk across the grass flats to the diver down boat at low tide.

There wasn't much to be found, but people had definitely been on the little sandy mound. He looked around carefully and went to get back in the boat when a little golden flash caught his eye. He bent over to carefully pick up the casing to a .25 automatic shell. He spent more than an hour minutely searching, but he couldn't find another.

A commercial fisherman went by as he was pushing the boat off and he waved, but was ignored. Jim's boat was a hell of a lot faster than the net boat, so he ran it down and held up his badge. The mullet fisherman stopped.

"I only need some information," he explained, yelling over the motor noise. "I'm out here to investigate the murder last Friday.

"There was an aluminum boat anchored out by that shell island (pointing) on the northern end with divers' flags set around. Did you see it?"

The fellow stared blankly at him a few seconds, shook his head and said, "Ain't no water there. Warn't no diver."

"I know it," Nick replied, patiently. "The killer left the boat there to take in. I want to know if you saw it."

"I ain't fishin' Friday. Didn't see nothin' at all."

"Who has the white lift front? Net boat."

"That stupid-ass thing looks like it wants to take off? Try John Putts. He's from Michigan. Don't know how to fish and ain't got sense to learn."

"Know where I can find him?"

"Back mouth of Sairy Creek north, prolly."

"Much obliged," Nick said, as he put the boat into gear. The chart showed him Sarah's Creek, so he'd find it quickly enough.

The white lift front was there, a man chatting with a woman in a green net boat with a boom light. He motored in close, avoiding the cork line carefully.

"John Putts?" he called.

"Yo! What?" the man in the lift front called back.

"I'm Nick Storie. Police. I'm here investigating the murder out here last Friday. Some people saw your boat about three thirty or so and maybe saw your friend's, too.

I need some information."

"I saw the boat they found blood in grounded on the little sandbar," Putts replied. "Maybe a quarter to four. I went by them and can't say if there were two or three people there, but I think it was only two. A man and a woman. I told that patrol clown all about it."

"Oh? Not our `Just the facts, Ma'am' expert?" Nick asked, flashing his most winning grin.

He got the grin back. "Ain't he a load?"

"I don't care about the island. There was an aluminum boat, a fourteen footer, maybe, anchored out by the gulf island on the north end. It had divers' flags around."

"Yeah. There wasn't anybody around. They probably left it with the flags so nobody'd mess with it. I went by about two hunnert feet off to eastward, but only gave it a quick once-over. That's a good spot to strike, but there weren't any fish there much. I saw it there, if that's important."

"It could be. I think the killer left it there earlier and used it to make a getaway."

"I sawr some fancy woman pullin' ut in thar," the woman on the green boat said. "She were comin' out'n fourteen. Sawr it there later on."

"You saw a woman taking it out there? She was pulling it?" Nick asked, trying to control his growing excitement. "Can you describe her? Could you identify her if called on?"

"Jist some woman. Sorta tallish. Couldn't see none've 'er much. Wearin' a yeller slicker'n a big hat."

"You're certain it was a woman?"

"Ain't no man got no legs like that'n!" She grinned, showing him a surprisingly good set of teeth. "Built like a brick shithouse, 's Putts'ud likely say.

"She were pullin' thet thar Johnboat 'long'th a beat old Glaspar. White'n 'uth sorta faded red trim. Hain't got no state numbers on't."

"OK. Two other quick questions. What time was it? Where's this fourteen?"

"'Uz mebbe sevenish or seven fifteen Friday mornin'n mouth fourteen's thet creek 'bout half a mile south.Got a old post standin' out'n ut used to have the number fourteen on a old board nailed to ut. We calls ut fourteen.

"Shaller. Careful if ya takes thet rig up't! Tide's goin' out. Get stuck'n gotta wait six – eight hours afore ut gets water tuh get out'n there."

"I might have to call on you two as witnesses when I break this case, okay?"

"Pays 'er gas'n time?"

"Not much, but the state pays mileage and a few dollars a day compensation"

"Can't be no worse'n what mullet's been bringin' in! Thet fancy woman been the killer?"

"It sure looks like it," Nick said, and waved as he backed out. He wrote down the numbers of their boats, then went back to ask, "What's your name? I didn't get it. I'm Nick."

"I'm Sweet Maggie Malone, believe't er not! He's Putts."

Nick waved again and motored back toward number fourteen. Maybe things were coming around at last! If either boat was found, they could probably trace it to somebody specific.

After forty five minutes of searching Nick located a runnel mouth with an old channel marker post standing out from it a hundred or so yards. The depth finder showed holes with washbars between them to the inside of the first curve, so he trimmed the motor up and went in slowly. The mangroves came almost together about a quarter mile in, but he managed to work the boat through to find himself sitting in a kidney-shaped bay that covered about three hundred acres. There were runnels coming in on either end, but he went as close to the mangroves as he could all the way around to be sure there were no others, then went into the southernmost runnel. About six hundred yards farther along, the runnel opened into another oval bay, perhaps fifty acres in area. There was a runnel that poured into it in back, so he went up that one for nearly another quarter mile, but the brown water kept getting shallower and branching into the reeds and mangroves. If his compass was right, he wasn't getting any closer to solid ground anywhere.

He went back to the large bay and up into the other channel. It was narrow but fairly deep and the current, with the tide going out, was fairly strong, indicating a lot of water farther in.

He crossed several small bays, while staying to the deeper flowing channel. He was in about two miles when he noticed cattails and flags along the bank.

Fresh water! This was a creek! It led into higher land!

Soon there were tall cabbage palms and low willow trees spotted here and there above the mangroves and back a few yards, so he was in an area where there was access to the creek from inland. There was quite a lot of saw grass, and ahead were willows that hung down over to virtually close off the little creek.

He cut the engine to study the banks – and heard a faint horn to his left. North. He listened intently a few minutes and heard a loud motorcycle moving at a high rate of speed. It was on a highway to be moving that fast. He'd estimate it was about a mile away.

The boat moved into the dense willow overhang as he pushed it along with the oar. It might barely squeeze through – when it hit something solid.

He went to the front and looked down to see the console of a boat just under the surface.

Nick thought a minute, then dropped the grapple anchor into the submerged boat, caught it firmly and started his engine to back slowly out from the willow overhang. The boat moved along sluggishly until it was in view.

He cut the engine, untied the anchor line from Jim's boat, and poled to the shore, where he tied the anchor line to a limb. He moved Jim's boat downstream a few yards and used another line to tie it to a stunted willow, then slopped along the muddy bank to the anchor line.

It was slow work and exhausting, but he finally had the nose of the submerged boat up on the bank enough to see it was an old white Glaspar with red trim. The drain plug had been pulled, the boat set adrift, and it caught on the overhanging willows and sank.

Nick took a stout piece of rope from Jim's boat to tie the Glaspar firmly, took the anchor back, and turned on the CB to call, "Breaker Breaker one nine. Got a smokey or county mountie out there? Breaker, breaker."

"This be the one Blue Streak Demon, ten four on county mountie," came back.

"I'm Det. Lt. Nick Storie on homicide detail. All I have on this thing is CB. Can you call FMP and have them contact me?"

"Go to channel eleven," came back. "This be the one Water Rat. We monitor nine and nineteen out here."

"Ten four. Thanks," Nick replied, and switched channels. He waited a minute, then said, "Water Rat?"

"Yo! Go!".

"Are you familiar with fourteen?"

"Yo."

"I'm up near the north-end runnel about three and half miles. I can hear some traffic noises to my left, north, maybe a mile or mile and a half away. It's shallow and narrow. I have to get this rig out of here.

"I've located a sixteen foot white Glaspar with red trim. It was scuttled. I drug it aground and tied it. I have a witness who described such a craft. It was used in the Rinks murder.

"Can you get someone in here?"

"Ten four. I'll have an air boat in there in five minutes. You'd better get out of there fast, if you're not in a canoe, or you'll be stuck for hours. There's not much water between you and the gulf, now. The place you are is within a thousand yards of the saw grass flow pond at the head of Snakebite Creek.

"Get out to the lower bays, anyhow. The air boat can't pass you in there. I'll have him wait at the last bay until you go by. You're gonna have to paddle a couple of places now, so move as fast as you can."

"Ten four!" Nick said, and started easing Jim's boat down the creek. He had to push the boat across one shallow bar before the first bay. The air boat was waiting there and waved him to go on. He got on the CB and explained. They told him to get out as fast as he could – or he might not get out for more than ten hours, when the tide would be full enough to move.

He had to push the heavy boat across two more shallow spots. He was swearing on the last one because he wasn't sure he could get it across, but he managed it. He was exhausted again as he ran into the large lower bay to find the MP shallow-draft boat there. He chatted with them for a few minutes. They couldn't go any farther upstream in even that boat, but the air boat was carrying Paddy's lab crew to the Glaspar. The air boat pulled it upstream to a little ridge where a swamp buggy could get in close and Paddy was called.

Nick finally went out into the gulf, found deeper water and headed for home. He had plenty, so far, but he still

needed a few small items before it was sewed up completely. Those phone calls were the one thing that could do
it, but none of his suspects seemed to have *made* any calls
from out there.

"I see you've had a very busy day!" Marsha greeted, as Nick went into the office. "Paddy and Jim went with Tiny to check over that boat. Jim tells me that a Glaspar has the serial numbers stamped directly into the transom, so it doesn't matter if there aren't any state numbers.

"You got maybe a bunch of notes I can type up, huh? Do you? Huh? Pant! Pant! Huh?"

"Interested in this one?" Nick asked.

"I've read your case notes through yesterday. That lock on your desk takes ten seconds to open with a piece of wire and a penknife.

"This one reads like a soap opera! I wish I'd met that guy! I ever find Hank sleeping with any other woman I'll cut it *off* for him! None of those nutty women cared if he slept around?"

"No, I really don't think they did, in that way. They seemed to expect it of him. It doesn't make any sense to me, either, but I think they're all pretty sincere about it.

"I have four main suspects. There has to be some way to tie one of them to it."

"Four? I'd think you'd have forty!"

"Nope! I only have Amy Fletcher, Rita Gomez, June Cerf – and any other tall, dark-haired woman with a great shape who ever slept with him. That's four. You're tall and dark-haired. You ever sleep with him?"

"Me? I'm dark all over. Lorna Fields has to be on your little list. You've never spoken with Mel.

"Did you ever stop to think the hair might have been a wig?"

"Uh-huh! I even considered some guy dressed up as a woman, but nobody could have done that after the time the slacks were shed for the bathing suit. Nobody could have fooled Rinks for one minute that way, either. It wasn't Lorna, because two other people saw her on the boat with Mel."

"Not at the time the murder was committed."

"But it was *not* Lorna Jamie Prescott and Judy Platt saw out there with him."

"Okay. It was one of those three or who?"

"Al Terns' daughter, Ellen."

"What the...! You haven't even seen her and she's not even in the state!"

"I'm not all that sure of that. She's been described to me by three people as being a beauty and as having slept with Rinks. Al told me she was in Milwaukee and gave me her address and phone number. I've called her several times and get a machine. She isn't there.

"I've traced two others, Kitty and Eileen. I got to both of them within a couple of hours."

"Wouldn't Al have recognized his own daughter on that boat that close?"

"He said the woman looked familiar, somehow, but he didn't know why. She was bundled up like that maybe so HE wouldn't recognize her?"

"Well, here's the lists of what was found at his place." She handed him a file folder. "You might want to go over it yourself. The new owners won't arrive here until tomorrow, so nothing's been touched, yet. You'd know more about what to look for than the crew."

"I think I'll go over there on my way home. Give the keys to Jim, will you? Tell him I filled the tank on the county's bill. I was using it for official business.

"I will be thoroughly *damned*! Here's a spent shell casing from a twenty five automatic I found out by the island! It was that one just inside the long barrier island I marked on the chart. I forgot it until I reached in my pocket just now! It's bagged, but it won't have anything after being under salt water for so long. Maybe a pin mark Tiny can use, or his ballistics department.

"I also found a couple of witnesses about the divers' boat out there. It's all in the notes. They know they could be called to testify.

"I'll spend tomorrow morning trying to find which of those calls are of any significance. I'm much too tired to worry about it now."

"The diver's boat? The witnesses? The casing from the murder shot?" Marsh said, wide-eyed. "What the Sam hell else has slipped whatever passes for your mind?"

He grinned and went out.

There was probably nothing in Rinks' house that would help with the case. Nick didn't think so from the first, or he'd have gone to the house while he was out there, anyhow, before the crew got there to move everything around.

He went through it very carefully, looking over the papers he found in a drawer in the kitchen and pocketing the book of addresses and phone numbers next to the phone. He found a stack of letters in a desk drawer in a remodeled bedroom. The room was furnished with a long writing/ computer desk along one side and contained a lot of electronic musical instrumentation and several sets of drums.

He shoved the letters into a paper bag to take along to read later, then checked the computer disks, but they seemed to be some kind of music programs he didn't begin to understand.

Rinks had been a hell of a lot neater than most bachelors, but still not too extreme. The place was clean, but it was disordered. He couldn't tell if anyone had been searching there before him – like maybe the murderer – looking for some incriminating clue.

He finally sighed heavily, shook his foggy head and headed for home. He was in that state of physical exhaustion that makes sleep impossible, so he turned on the TV for awhile and tried to forget the case. After about two hours he went to bed and was able to finally drop off.

"The old boat was last registered to a Marvin Randall Shackleford in Starke, Florida," Paddy reported the next morning, when Nick and Jim went into his office for a briefing. "Shackleford gave it to some kids to fix up. They patched the small crack in the bottom and sold it to `some old guy in a rusty old brown Ford pickup for twenty bucks.

"That's all we have. The kids sanded the FL numbers off and repainted it. That was done eight years ago. The boat was launched a couple hundred feet from the Trail across the saw grass. There's a rough limestone road a little way into the swamp there that canoe fishermen use. We could trace where the boat crushed the grass in spots.

"The aluminum job would be easier to get in and out than the Glaspar. Nobody saw anything, for certain, but some kids who live a couple miles farther out said there was an old car parked there all day Friday."

"How did she get the car there?" Nick asked.

"The Trailways bus stops at a filling station one and three quarter miles back this way," Paddy said. "We checked with all the drivers. There's always someone in charge there, and they picked up several women, but none who would fit our descriptions. One driver said he saw a woman walking toward Naples at about nine ten carrying a yellow gas can, but she waved him on when he slowed. He said all he remembered about her was that she was wearing a yellow rain slicker and fishing boots – and a big straw hat."

"Very clever!" Nick said. "That was her. She leaves the old car there and takes a ride with the first out of state tourist heading north. No witness!"

"You're fairly sure?" Jim asked.

"The fisherman – or fisher*woman* – saw her pulling the aluminum boat out. She was wearing a big straw hat and a rain slicker, but no boots."

"What kind of old car?" Marsha asked. "The one the kids saw parked there Friday morning."

"It was rust brown and one of those square things from the early seventies or late sixties," Paddy answered. "They say they didn't get close. I suppose they don't steal things out of old wrecks like that."

"Paddy! How cynical!" Jim laughed. "True, but cynical.

"What do we look for?"

"Why would she know about that place at all?" Nick asked. "None of my suspects is the type to run around swamps to ever know about such a place in case she ever needed it, and how in hell would she know the creek leads into the gulf?

"Damn it! I *know* this case is laid out and crystal clear! I just can't read it! I'm missing something obvious!"

"Maybe the one you haven't met yet is the outdoorsy type," Marsha suggested. "I tried calling the number, and only got an answering machine."

"Well, if we get a call back sometime this afternoon I'll really get suspicious of her," Nick said, grimly. "That would be timing with a little too much coincidence thrown in. The problem with that is it would throw my main suspect out of the whole thing.

"Well, maybe not that much. I have some other things to check out. Maybe the answer'll turn up in this crap. I have the tedious part to go through now. I hate the working from a list part.

"I'll have to solve this one before Saturday. I have a date."

"Say! Maybe Janet knew Rinks! She's tall, has a great shape and has long dark hair!" Marsha said, leering evilly.

"Hey, now, you! There are *some* things we don't joke about!" Nick retorted. "Say! Marsha, get me the missing vehicle report for the past two weeks."

Ed Goins came in and Paddy said he'd remain in charge of the night shift for another day or two. Jim, Marsha and Nick went back to their respective desks. Paddy went into his office with Ed.

Nick dropped the sack of letters from Rinks' house on his desk and dropped the phone/address book in the drawer, poured a cup of coffee, and sat to look through them.

He hated reading other people's mail. These were mostly from women who were asking for his advice of a nature he found too embarrassingly personal in nature. Kitty, Eileen and Ellen wrote to Rinks sporadically. There wasn't very much in the letters that could damage them when you considered that everyone knew they'd slept with him. The letters weren't very erotic. They either asked for his advice or thanked him for advice already given.

He put one aside from someone who merely signed the letter with "Corrie". She told about a skiing trip to Colorado, then: *I know what you meant in your last letter about your problem. I hope you can make her understand your feelings about that kind of situation. She is not reacting rationally, because you would never do anything to hurt her with him.*

Bill, she has to understand your position. No one who knows you would believe you would ever do those things. She is acting like a true paranoid type of person. Are you sure she isn't using some drug like cocaine?

I don't know her very well, but if she doesn't come to her senses soon I will try to talk to her...

There was no date and no envelope and there was no name except "Corrie".

So everything was not quite so perfect with everybody in this! Some woman was "acting like a true paranoid" where Rinks was concerned!

Apparently a boyfriend (Or husband? Maybe she'd told him she wasn't married?) was onto him and was causing her trouble of some sort.

Ellen always ended her letters with a suggestion he come to live with her, but so did several others.

This was the first lead not connected to the case by the events surrounding the actual killing. It could be important, or it could be another big fat zero.

Nick sighed and read the rest of the letters, then opened the file Marsha left on his desk. Rinks' bank statements were normal, except for one item. A couple of hundred dollars a month to some woman in Louisiana.

He kept all his canceled checks and the deposit receipts in a box in the desk drawer. He was most definitely not being blackmailed, nor had he been receiving any blackmail-type payments. He made a lot of money (compared to a cop's salary) and he gave a lot of it away, but nothing to any pattern. No sudden large sums going in either direction, no mysterious checks on the third Friday of every month for an even five thousand dollars.

Nothing.

His IRS forms were exact to the last penny. He was, apparently, a rare truly honest type. There was a sheet in the back of the bank statements file explaining that the two hundred dollars a month was for child support. Rinks was helping to pay for the raising of a biracial young boy.

There were no records of the child's birth.

Maybe Rinks had fathered a child who would inherit. That point would have to be checked. He called over to Marsha to ask her to start the wheels turning on that.

Nick sighed again and sat back, then picked up the address book to try to locate Corrie, but found nothing.

There was one page missing from the book! A Dorine Carlson was followed by a Laurie Dodd! There was a little fuzz down between the pages where it had been torn out, carefully. That could merely be a coincidence. It could be a deliberate attempt to divert suspicion onto the one suspect who was in that part of the alphabet, June Cerf — after all, it would be perfectly natural for him to have both her numbers. He worked at the restaurant with the band. Nothing else in the book caught his attention. There wasn't anything for it now but to start trying to find something in that SS and cellular phone list.

He dreaded that! A vitally important answer was definitely somewhere in that, but what? None of those calls originated from a phone registered to *any* of the suspects.

He also had to connect how the killer knew about the place where she launched the boats. That a woman could do it, he didn't doubt. A trailer with a winch and that light aluminum boat. She could have dropped the motor from the old Glaspar into the aluminum job, then cranked the whole thing up. The only hard part would be getting the Glaspar across the grass in the first place, but there had been enough rain to have made the little saw grass lake a couple of inches deeper on Thursday. That's all it would take. The creek would drop the water level in a few hours.

He called the airport weather station for the record. There had been one and a half inches of rain, with only a light southwesterly wind south of Naples along the coast Thursday morning. That was another little item for his chart.

Marsha came over to hand him a computer readout of the vehicles reported stolen recently. She'd painted a yellow highlighter on one item: "1968 Chrysler Imperial, Brown, four door. Stolen from U Partem Auto Salvage, Immokalee, Thursday, May 7, 1992. Vehicle was outside the wall and was in good running condition. Needed only a battery. Stolen between 8:00 PM and 11:00 PM. VIN # ...."

"You think maybe that was our square old brown car?" Nick asked.

"Read all about it on the next page, Sherlock," Marsha suggested, grinning.

The highlight there: "1968 Chrysler Imperial, VIN # ... found abandoned in wooded area of Golden Gate May 13, 1992, traced to the...."

"Paddy went to check it a few minutes ago," she said. "Want to bet?"

"Nope! Not even maybe! We're closing in on this one, Marsh. If I can find a couple more things, we've got our killer."

"Well, it's past my lunch time. Take me out and I'll help with those numbers."

"You're on!" Nick agreed.

"Hi! Here's Tiny's forensic report on the car," Marsha said upon returning to her desk from lunch. "Want to see it?"

Nick took the pages and glanced at them. He noted the more important things, such as the fact the car had a trailer hitch with a small utility trailer ball in it.

For pulling a boat trailer?

The ball was scarred from recent use. There were no fingerprints in the car other than those of the regular people working at the junkyard. The last driver apparently wore soft (cotton?) gloves that smudged over everything on the steering wheel, the gearshift buttons and anything else touched.

Nick flipped on through the report, then asked Marsha to buzz Tiny on the interphone.

He came on.

"Tiny? Have you printed the battery box and hood latch on that old Chrysler?"

"The hood latch. We didn't print the battery itself, no. Why?"

"When that car was stolen, it didn't have a battery. It had a battery when you checked it?"

"Hang on!" Tiny cried, and Nick could hear him yelling for somebody to get back to that car and to very carefully remove the battery without touching it and bring it in to the lab. Yesterday!

"It's an older used battery," Tiny finally said. "We can hope. I didn't have anything to make me think of it. Thanks for the tip. Probably saved my ass."

"There are several cars in running order in the front of that yard," Marsha said. "I called them. They sell the ones they have clear titles for to collectors. They leave out the batteries and put the keys over the visor."

"So we've got a very concise picture of everything – except for who pulled the trigger," Nick mused. "I keep getting the feeling it's all there staring us in the face. I haven't put all the figures into the right columns yet."

He went to sit at his desk to enter the pieces about the car into his notes in their proper spots. He always made a sort of chart of boxes he could fill in. The order of squares took him moment by moment through the crime, the entry was made when the evidence was tight.

His phone buzzed and he reached for it, glancing up to

see Marsha staring oddly at him.

"Storie," he said.

"Lt. Storie? This is Ellen Terns. I have several messages on my machine to please call you?"

He was almost dumbfounded, but made a fast recovery. "I've been trying to reach you for several days. I have some bad news, if you haven't heard, and I need to ask you a question or two."

"Bad news? Is Dad all right?!"

"He's fine. This is about Bill Rinks."

"Bill? I don't understand."

"I'm afraid I have the extremely unpleasant duty to inform you he's dead. He was murdered," Nick said, not quite knowing which direction to take this. He waited into the stunned silence for a few moments, then, "Miss Terns?"

"Oh, dear God in heaven! Tell me this is some kind of insane sick joke!"

"I'm afraid not. I'm sorry. I learned from your father that you dated Mr. Rinks and must know if you are aware of *any* fact, any smallest fact whatever, that could help us in finding a direction to take in this kind of investigation. It seems Mr. Rinks was liked by everyone he met."

"I have to call Dad! I know he's been trying to call, but he won't leave a message on the machine. He just hangs up if I don't.... Oh, God!

"Not Bill! Please! Not Bill!"

"Miss Terns, if you know of anything, no matter how small, we *must* know!"

"I don't believe you! No one would hurt Bill!

"I'll get control of myself in just a minute. I have to! Just give me a minute to think."

"Where have you been for the past few days? You should leave an emergency number with someone. A message about how to contact you. Can't you call your phone and get your messages?"

"I was in New York for a shoot. This won't sink in. It won't.

"What happened? When?"

"A shoot?"

"I'm modeling for Crest Cosmetic Arts International. Would it be better if I called Dad?"

"He's probably very worried he can't reach you. Maybe if you could tell me when...."

She hung up!

Nick looked at Marsha, who had been listening to the whole conversation on her extension. She shrugged and said, "I'll call the agency, but she was really there or she wouldn't have dared to say she was. *She* ain't it!"

Nick sighed for the ten thousandth time for the day and sat back to think. Anything to keep from doing what he knew he'd have to do, now. Those lists of phone numbers were the tedium that often made this kind of work less than pleasant.

Another sigh, then he picked up the list. It was times and caller ID codes with the destination numbers on the first of several sheets, then a sheet of the numbers and who they were registered to on another. That second one was easily the biggest disappointment, so far, because none of the numbers was registered to anyone he knew to be involved in the case.

"Marsh?" he called. "Can you get me cellular numbers for all the businesses ... wait. I have a listing in here somewhere ... here it is. Hmmm. J. Prescott has a cellular car phone.... Cerf's Surf has a cellular *and* car phone.... Mel Sharpe has a cellular car phone. Rita Gomez has one and Amy Fletcher has one.

"Why in *Hell* would every damned suspect in this stupid

mess have one of the miserable damned things?!"

"Because they're all in the higher brackets and a cellular phone's a status symbol," Marsha replied, putting a cup of black coffee on his desk and pulling up a chair. "I think they ought to outlaw the things! Have you seen the way some people drive while they're chatting away?

"As for that point, what do you think of that stupid ad on TV?"

"Marsh, what in the hell are you talking about?"

"That cell phone ad. Some idiot's wife is having a baby, she's in the car, moaning – and he's calling the hospital on his handy-dandy cell phone – while backing out of his driveway onto a busy street! The phone's in one hand, a pregnant woman moaning on the seat next to him, driving a car backward out into a busy street with one hand while looking over the back of the seat!

"What do you think of the ads telling how powerful Rising Sun Motors' new Super Turbocharged V-six can pass a big tanker truck in a flash – going up a blind hill on a blind curve?

"Crazy, man! What a thrill! Did you ever notice the ad about most sinus medicines making you drowsy, but Brand X doesn't? Then why is it that the doofus who took the crud being advertised was driving on the wrong side of the road when she had to swerve to miss the one who took the sleep-inducing garbage – who was driving normally?

"The morons who come up with those ads are on crack, right?"

"You sure are wound up. Here. Look for any of these numbers on those sheets and I'll check these." He handed her half the printouts.

Forty minutes later they had nothing. Zilch. None of their numbers were called or made calls in the area.

"Well? Now what?" Marsha asked.

"Damn it all, Marsh! We *know* she made several calls out there! We *know* ... wait a minute! We know she made one at about three o'clock from the end of the channel into Royal Rubbish Acres. I have to get the numbers from right there at that time, then we match them to this list and we have a very good start.

"I'm on my way to the phone company. My court order will cover it."

"There's another possibility," Marsha cautioned. Nick raised his eyebrows at her.

"Did it ever occur to you she may not have actually made any calls?"

"Uh-huh. I don't want to think about that. She might have made it a point to be seen talking on a cell phone out there by several people so we'd try to trace the calls and come up with nothing or the wrong suspect. If we tried to base a case on phone calls, we'd have to produce records of those calls, or the case would collapse. That's why I've put the calls to the side, so to speak. I'm building the case from several angles. If the phone thing falls through it's not going to hurt us, I promise!"

Marsha gave him the victory "V" sign and a tight grin, then started pushing the sheets back into the file.

Nick left.

"What I have to find is what calls were made from this area, area S twelve on your map, between a quarter to three and three thirty PM on Friday afternoon," Nick explained to the arrogant jerk, "Mr. Elton Hobbs – Flr. Sup." according to the little name tag on his pocket, at the phone company's main billing offices. "This is a capital murder investigation. This is a court order."

"Serve it on the cellular carriers, then!" the jackass Nick was talking to snapped.

"I'm serving it on you," Nick said, silkily. "If you fail to comply with this order your tail cools a cell for contempt of court, capich?"

"Ship to shore and marine cellular calls do *not* go through this office!"

"The billing does, and that's the fastest way to get what we need."

"Tough shit! Some hotshot *flatfoot* doesn't scare *me*!" the ass retorted. "You might want to try to prove *that* one to a judge! I'm busy!"

Nick yanked the cuffs from his belt and slapped one side on his wrist and the other to the jerk.

"You are under arrest on the charge of contempt of lawfully executed court order A five seven four four dash six six seven nine. You have the right to remain silent. Should you choose to give up that right...."

"Hey! Hey! What the hell do you think you're doing?!" Hobbs yelled.

Other people were coming to stare in the door. One woman winked and gave Nick a "Thumbs up." Apparently Flr. Sup. Mr. Elton Hobbs wasn't too popular with his underlings.

"I'm arresting you for contempt of court. Now you go downtown for the booking, fingerprinting and mug shots, then you go before Judge Collins to explain why you defied her order in a capital murder case.

"Let's see ... if you give up that right anything you say can and will be used against you in a court of law. You have the right of an attorney's presence during any questioning. If you cannot afford one the court will appoint one.

"Do you understand these rights?

"Okay then! Let's go! I think you'll *really* enjoy the strip and body cavity searches!"

"But I don't *have* the stuff you want here! This is crazy! That stuff isn't even *here*!"

"That's funny. It was a matter of only a few seconds down in the Everglades City branch. You see, I'm going to produce the readouts from down there for the judge, which will prove beyond any reasonable doubt that you *do* have the stuff here, and that all you're doing is pulling an act to impress these people – which I'm sure you did, but not the way you planned. I think ninety days in a cell ought to give you plenty of time to think it over, don't you?

"Let's go!"

"I'm not going anywhere!"

"Oh, good! You're resisting arrest! Want to take a swing at me? That makes it a felony. Resist with violence, you know."

"What is going on in here?" a woman asked, coming in through the crowd at the door.

"Mrs. Stewart! This damned *flatfoot* is trying to arrest me!" Elton whined.

"Trying to? Oh, come *on*! I just *did*!" Nick pointed out.

"What's going on here, officer?" she asked.

Nick handed her the court order, and said, "Mr. Hobbs refuses to comply. I'm taking him in for booking."

"What do you need from us here, officer?"

Nick repeated what he needed.

"Angela! Get me a printout from cell billing. Area S twelve from fourteen forty five to sixteen hundred thirty on the eighth of this month. SS and C one and two," she said to a girl near the door. "Officer, if you would release Mr. Hobbs in my custody, I will fully assure you this kind of thing will never happen again. Our policy is to always cooperate with law enforcement agencies. Mr. Hobbs has embarrassed the company. He will not have a second chance to do that."

"You stupid goddamned dyke bitch!" Hobbs screamed. "You think you're so hot! Big bad boss over us men! You've been waiting to get me! You know damned well you stole my promotion! You've always been out to get me!"

"To tell the truth, I have," she agreed quietly. "You are and always were unqualified for your position.

"Officer?"

Nick grinned at her and unlocked the handcuffs. Angela returned with several pages of printout. Nick thanked Mrs. Stewart and left. Elton was fuming and cursing everyone in the company who let "a bunch of bull dykes take a man's job!" This case was weird, but he was getting used to it. A cop came across all types. Elton Hobbs was going to be looking for a job in a saturated labor market – and he was *not* going to find one in management.

"I'll compare these cellphone numbers," Marsha suggested. "If any of them match, we can use it. If not, we know it was a ruse.

"Paddy and Tiny are in the gloom room right now. Jim's in, and Ed."

Nick nodded, and went on into Paddy's office. "Anything I need to know?"

"No. No prints on the battery," Tiny replied. "It's been wiped. It's a little lawnmower battery, anyhow."

"Lawnmower battery? Would that start that big car?"

"Yo. They have gear-driven starters on Chrysler products, It would eat the battery up after awhile, but it would work a few times.

"There was some gasoline with two-cycle oil spilled on the rear floorboard between the rear and front seats, so the gas can was carried there. The Glaspar had green algae growing below the natural water line, so it had been in the water for at least a week before Friday."

"Crap. I'd hoped it was launched on Thursday when the extra rainwater filled the saw grass pond."

"It was. The algae was scraped from going across the grass. It was moved from somewhere else."

"I don't think so," Jim argued. "I think it was left up at that end of the pond, which means the murder was planned at least a week before."

"I'll have to go back out there and look around," Nick said. "I'll need a map to get me to the exact spot. I also need the names of those kids. The ones who saw the car on Friday."

"You do?" Paddy asked.

"Did you ask them if they'd seen the Glaspar somewhere else around that pond?"

Jim grinned. Paddy shook his head.

"You stated you very much wanted to know how the killer even knew about that place," Ed said. "I didn't have much to do last night and had to go through some county records, so I had them print out the tax records for the whole area. Maybe you'll recognize a name on it. I put the printout on your desk."

"Thanks, Ed. That'll save me a lot of time."

There wasn't anything else for Nick, so he went to his desk to look over the tax records. He didn't recognize anything there, but put the lists with the rest of his paper-work.

Marsha handed him a listing with nine numbers that had called from both areas in the gulf within the time-frames. He didn't see anything, so said he was going hunting in the reed swamps. Marsha shook her head and grinned.

"You've had a complaint filed against you. Some guy named Hobbs claims that you beat him up and threatened him with arrest without cause.

"I told him Internal Affairs' number and said to make certain he had backup witnesses because you could charge him with making a false complaint if he was shown to be acting in spite."

"I don't need any IA investigation right now!" Nick snapped.

"I assured him you would never file those charges against him without being able to prove due cause, so he could go ahead and file his complaint." She grinned.

"Okay! What *did* you tell him I'd do?"

"Oh, I said you always had the option of suing the piss out of him for a false claim that indicated, as his complaint implied, that you had made any physical assault on him without provocation. I then explained what provocation is. I don't think you'll be hearing anything more out of your *dear* friend, Hobbs!"

"What is provocation?".

"In this case?" she answered, with a giggle. "Anything like resisting a lawful court order would place him under criminal contempt, which would mean you could arrest him with whatever force you deemed necessary. If he resisted arrest in any violent way you could go so far as to blow his stupid head off for him!

"I explained that resisting arrest was filed either without violence or with violence. If it was without violence he could only get a few months in the pen. If he took a swing at you you were free to do anything you wanted. I also told him if you had given him his rights, he was under arrest, and that he remained under that arrest until you officially released him. Personally. No one else could do that.

"He said you released him in Mrs. Stewart's custody, so I said, so long as you directly stated you were releasing him from arrest, he was out of that part of it, but if you merely allowed Mrs. Stewart to take over without formally stating that he was released he was still under arrest, legally."

"So what?"

"Why, I explained that you could come pick him up anytime in the next two years for any reason whatever, such as if you were in a lousy mood or maybe just PO'ed about phone solicitors calling every night when you were trying to fix your supper, or getting in the shower, or something. The charges he was arrested on remain active for *two whole years!*

"He's a total nutcase. I'm glad he didn't know I'm black. It was bad enough that a stupid bull dyke was handling a man's job there."

"He seems to have a problem about a female boss. He was trying to show the staff there how to handle a common flatfoot. It backfired, and he doesn't have the brains to drop it. The whole world's conspiring to make him look like the fool he is. There's going to be some other kind of trouble from that one. Count on it!

"I'm going out to the pond. I'll stop in before the end of the day. I have a little idea to try out.

"I keep saying we have to cover all the angles and we've been looking at the phone calls from the wrong one.

"Later!" He went out to his car.

Nick had to walk in from just a few yards from the Tamiami Trail. His car wasn't designed to go into that kind of morass. He could see where swamp buggies had come through, and even found one spot where the Chrysler had driven out. The big heavy car wouldn't stick with the solid lime rock undersurface only a few inches below, and the suspension would handle the pounding. If the boat hadn't been tied down tight it would get beat up on the light trailer, but she probably went out dead slow through the bad parts.

The shallow saw grass pond stretched out for several acres. It had a webbing of narrow ditch-like channels running through it, making Nick wonder how she got to that boat if it was left out there anywhere.

The bus driver said she was wearing fisherman's boots. Hip boots!

The bottom had an inch or two of light sticky mud. It was basically lime rock under that, so she probably simply waded to wherever the boat was kept.

He sighed and dropped anything the water might damage into an evidence bag and sealed it, shoved it into his shirt pocket, and slipped into the muddy water, taking a six foot piece of thin branch from the edge of the path to feel for the depth ahead of him. Mostly, it was less than eighteen inches.

After about another hour and a half of slogging among the shallow channels while fighting through the razor-like saw grass he found an old willow stump with wear marks from a rope around it. The Glaspar could have been tied there and wouldn't be visible from the pathway where people could come in. There was still a slight shallow triangular groove into the bank right up to the stump. He'd have trouble getting back to that exact spot unless he could mark it.

Nick was resourceful. He attached his white handkerchief to the stick he was carrying and stood it alongside the stump base. He pushed it in as far as it would go, but it still tended to fall over. There was rock less than a foot under the surface of the soggy soil.

The saw grass was as tough as rope. He used his penknife to cut and weave a cord and tied the stick to the stump. It was solid.

He went back out to the path. When he looked back he

could see the white of the handkerchief about ten inches above the saw grass.

There wasn't anything else to see, so he sloshed back to his car, got an old rubberized tarp out of the trunk to cover the seat, and climbed in to radio for Tiny to send someone out with a canoe to take a cast of the indentation in the bank and some pictures of the stump.

"Why do we need the print cast?" Tiny asked.

"Because it's going to fit the nose of that Glaspar pulled out of the creek. Exactly. It's another small detail, but you know how I am. If there's ever any question I want to be able to prove *that* boat was tied to *that* stump."

"You do worry about those details. You'll have your cast."

Another little box filled in on his chart.

Nick backed out and rechecked the addresses Paddy gave him. He drove back to where he found three preteenage boys working on a log playhouse on the higher bank of the canal near where one of the kids on Paddy's list lived, so he called, "Juan? Juan Oliviez?"

All three came to stare at him.

"You should take off your pants when you go swimming, man!" one of them said. "I'm Juan. What you want?"

"I'm a cop. Nick.

"I need to know if any of you saw the old fiberglass boat they pulled out of the creek before?"

"Old man Pickleface put it there," one of them said. "He put it there every year. He tied it to a pipe or somethin'."

"Old man Pickleface?"

"Yeah. We call him Ol' Pickleface," Juan said. "He's really dumb, man! That cruddy boat's too big for in there!"

"Yeah! He told us if anybody touched his boat he'd have us in jail," another said. "Stupido! Like he could have us put in jail just because somebody touched his stupid boat?

Right, man!"

"You don't know his name, I guess?"

"He's always Ol' Pickleface," Juan replied. "Real old! Stingy cheap bastard. Anybody else'd give us a buck or two to see nobody fucked with his boat."

"What kind of car did he drive?"

"Old rusty Ford truck that looks like it won't make it to town and back," Juan said. "Cheap old bastard got money up his ass and won't even buy a good car."

"He use the boat for fishing?"

They looked at each other, shrugged, and said they'd never seen him take any fishing equipment out with him. He didn't live anywhere around there.

Curiouser and curiouser. Nick made a few notes and sat to consider for a minute before driving slowly back toward the station for Marsha to fuss over his being wet and cold.

"Cold?! It's eighty eight degrees out there! I wasn't cold until I came in here where you keep it at about forty five degrees!

"Marsha? Why was that damned boat out there, and what did Old Pickleface use it for? More importantly, how did our killer know about it?"

"What, besides fishing, is there to do in a boat out there? Run drugs?" she returned.

"That far in? In those conditions? When he couldn't get in or out more than two thirds of the time?"

"Maybe there's a pot patch in there? The kids did say he put it there every year."

"Damn! Now I have to do anoth ... no I don't! That isn't my case! No way! Call the DEA and make a suggestion they check anywhere he could go in that boat from in there. I have to worry about a murder, not pot.

"Still, how did our murderer know about the boat at all? None of my suspects are, as so aptly noted, the outdoorsy types who would ever go 'way out there to plod around in a dirty swamp for any reason I can picture.."

"She might have gone out there with somebody else for some reason or other. Maybe her boyfriend hunts frogs out there. I heard some of them do that."

"But there isn't anything out there! Nothing but miles and miles of swamp! Frogs, you can get in the ditches by the road. Why go to that much trouble?"

"Then she went out there specifically to see a swamp. It's what you have. Eliminate the impossible and go with what's left. That's all that's left.

"So why would anyone want to see a swamp?"

"Maybe somebody sold a.... Maybe.... I've got this lovely swamp to sell you, cheap! It's not *always* a joke — especially to anyone who's *bought* one of those famous Florida swamps! Ed even supplied me with nice tax plots."

"Except Rinks didn't sell anybody any Florida swamp or anything else." Marsha reminded.

"Ah! Maybe he knew who *did*! Maybe a little bit of motive's finally coming through this thing!"

He sat and took out the tax rolls to pour over them. He had to get a plot map sent over so he'd know where each holding was.

It was all held by various companies, what little wasn't state land. That meant another round of tedium, pouring over the charters.

"The angle! I almost forgot about that little point!" he suddenly cried. "Marsh, hand me those phone lists. Something just rang a bell. A phone bell!"

"There's one other little juicy item you may want to hear about," Marsha said. "Your friend Elton Hobbs?

"Mrs. Stewart charged him with felony assault and battery and will prosecute, as she puts it, `Until Satan passes by my back door on snowshoes!'

"It seems she was explaining to the personnel manager about his behavior. He called her a few choice and very unflattering epithets, then took a swing at her. She crowned him with the marble pen set from the manager's desk. Concussion city! He's under a fifteen grand bond."

"Well! *Some*thing went right today!" Nick said brightly.

Nick was seated at his desk, comparing the various lists, while Marsha watched him with a concerned expression. She knew how he could have a set of facts hidden somewhere in his mind, and those facts would suddenly line up in such a way to make a case suddenly clear. That "phone bell" remark made her certain he'd done it again, but she could also see there was something missing. He was also going to get a surprise when he read the report from Louisiana.

He took out a sheet of paper to start listing events in chronological order. The switchboard lit up and Marsha went to work. Ed Goins came in and went directly to Nick with a couple of report forms. Nick looked up. "What you got, Ed?"

"I figured you'd want to trace the aluminum boat and had a little time. It's slow this time of year.

"I found it."

"I could kiss you!"

"I don't think my wife would approve, and I know quite surely I wouldn't," Ed said, seriously. Nick never quite knew when Ed was joking, but caught the little sparkle in his eye, and grinned. He took the reports.

"I sorted through the reports of all missing boats. It seems your murderer likes to steal things, so it seemed a logical step."

The first sheet was a missing vehicle report. It stated that a fourteen foot aluminum bass boat on a trailer had been stolen from Gadson's Fish Camp, who was a dealer in that brand of boat, along with a ten horsepower motor from another boat from in front of the camp between the hours of 1:00 AM and 2:30 AM Friday, May 8. The padlocks were cut off of the retainer chains, then the thief simply drove off with the boat. There was a lot of other information included, but that was basically it.

The second sheet was a merchandise recovery report that stated the boat and extra motor were found parked to the side of the camp on opening Saturday morning. No one knew when it was put back there, but it was after midnight Friday, when the camp was closed. A standard printing and evidence search was conducted, but no prints etc....

It was a total dead end. All they knew was the boat disappeared one night and was back the next. The working assumption was that someone unknown wanted to go fishing and didn't want to rent or buy a boat. The motor had been run in salt water.

"Thanks, Ed," Nick said. "This fills in a few gaps nicely. I have this case solved I think, but these little details tie things together in a noose around a killer's neck. Each new added detail's another loop!"

"If I may suggest, don't try to be poetic, Sir. You really aren't," Ed said, but this time he couldn't quite stop the flash of a grin.

Ed went into Paddy's office while Nick entered the times and dates on his chronological chart, then sat to think a moment.

The next step was the tax rolls. He found the parts he needed, then swung his computer monitor around and started asking the machine questions. He wasn't very good at it, so called Marsha over.

"Marsh, I need to find the ownership of corporations. I can find most of it, but not what I need."

"Give me an example."

"Clearblue Realty Brokers, Inc. They're on Paradise and Meadow Lark off Davis. Four seventeen."

She called up realty, which showed nine type listings on

the screen. She touched the box marked "Reg. Brokers" with the stylus, which brought up nine more boxes.

She asked what kind of brokers they were.

"I've no vaguest idea. Just listed as brokers on the tax rolls."

"Well? It's time to let your fingers do the walking!" She grinned, so he grabbed the phone book, flipped through to the yellow pages, and read out, "Wholesale, retail, large tracts, estate holdings and related investments."

She touched the stylus to "General" and a long list came on the screen. She scrolled down to "Clearblue Realty," which had four companies. She touched "Large tracts Dev."

"Clearblue Realty Holdings <Overview Land Trust Investors, Inc. <Hodgkinson Diversified."

She then touched the stylus to "Hodgkinson Diversified" and said, "So! It was the Cerf bitch. How you gonna prove it?"

Mr. Arnold Thomas Hodgkinson, sole prop./C.E.O. was on the screen.

"With a phone call. I have this one figured out, now. It's early enough no one will be there. I'll have to find a solid connection with only one number. I already have it with the other.

"Have Paddy and whoever else wants in on this one in Paddy's office in about ten minutes? Ed should be in on it."

He picked up the data sheet received from Louisiana, read it a moment and cried, "And *there's* my motive! Bigger than *Hell*, there's my *motive*!"

"Here's what I have right now, and what I think," Nick explained to Jim, Ed, Tiny, Marsha and Paddy. "It's really a very simple and sordid case. I thought almost from the very first day I knew who had killed Bill Rinks. I couldn't quite hook it together, though I had all the basics.

"I'm going to gamble that I'm right. I'll take you through every step of this thing, then call a number on the lists. If I'm right, the proof of how it was done will be the answer on that call.

"The thing started back a fairly long time ago, but we're involved in only the past few days, except for the motive. That's from almost twelve years ago. The killer was about to be exposed, or thought she was, as a scheming gold-digging bitch. To be exposed that way would cost her what she'd been working for, in her own way, all her life. She's engaged to marry a disgustingly wealthy old eccentric land developer. He's suspicious and cheap, but he can't live very much longer, even if she has to sort of speed the end.

"That tells you who the killer is. June Cerf.

"There was a detective following her. Her disgustingly wealthy old suitor does *not* trust her, even to the point he demanded a prenuptial agreement. She was about to get that marriage without the agreement, but Bill Rinks knew far too much and she was afraid he'd refuse to hide what he knew from the detective.

"The thing she desperately feared being exposed is that she's mother of an illegitimate child, born eleven years ago. Rinks knew all about it, because the father was the late `Hands' Bourbonne of New Orleans. Rinks was helping to support the kid from the time it was born. She wasn't. Rinks wasn't going to hide that fact from the private detective Hodgkinson had chasing her.

"If her eccentric millionaire sugar daddy ever learned she'd mothered an illegitimate child he'd probably drop her. If he learned the father was black he *damned* well would! The fact is, she felt Rinks could end her chance to marry tens of millions of dollars.

"She knew about the boat Hodgkinson, or Old Pickleface, kept in that grass pond because she'd been out there with him in it. The land to the south of that creek for nearly half a mile and back as far belongs to Clearblue Investments, which is owned by Hodgkinson. She also knew the creek went into the gulf. She knew the little channels across the pond. She knew about the trail in there.

"It wasn't hard to set up. She said she'd like to go out for a day to relax and talk or something. She knew the absolutely perfect place! Maybe she said she wanted to make arrangements to take care of her own *dear* little boy once she had all that money, so Rinks agreed to take her out.

"She set up the time, stole the car, and used an aluminum boat and two motors from Gadson's Fish Camp, figured the tide for getting in and out Friday morning, set everything up, and got the boat and motors back in time to prevent any great search for them. It was really a simple deal!"

"I can see you've got an answer to how she could appear to be in her office all that time," Paddy said. "Is that what the phone call's about?"

"Uh-huh! That's why she was on the phone out there all the time. Everything's recorded automatically on your phone here, so I'll show exactly how she did it."

"Yeah, but there weren't any calls from her cell phone from out there," Marsha said. "How did you figure that one?"

"There was a number called at three oh three from the canal at Royal Sludge Acres to the same number that three more calls were made later through Everglades City relay station. We were looking at the wrong end of that when we checked the lists.

"Did you notice one of those phones that made the calls from both places was registered to Clearblue Realty Brokers, Inc.?"

"Hodgkinson again!" Jim said. "She could get her hands on any of that stuff she wanted! Anytime!"

"Right! All those calls were made to (He picked up the phone on Paddy's desk and punched the numbers as he said them) five five five four one four seven. Ah!"

He switched on the open speaker. The number rang three times, then, "Miss Cerf is not in the office at the present time. Please leave a message at the tone. If you wish to speak to someone else and are calling from a touch-tone unit, you may now push three for the bar, four for the restaurant, five for the kitchen or six for the maitre D's station ... bleep!"

"Simple. She called her own unlisted number in her own office and punched for whichever place she wanted to raise hell in through the inside system. I could punch four and fire a waitress, three to raise all kinds of hell because of an order of twenty cases instead of two or anything else.

"The important thing is we have four calls to that unlisted number from cell phones out there in the gulf at the times the murderer was seen using a cell phone. No one in the restaurant could tell she wasn't making the calls directly from her office and no one dared to check. We have a complete easy access to who received those calls and when, so we can prove June Cerf made those calls.

"This is tight! If we didn't have one thing other than those calls we could prosecute this one. Details, like motive, are in the back instead of the front. It's been a case that's been more than a little bit weird all along."

"You don't seem to have missed any major details," Paddy said. "I'll get a warrant."

"I couldn't believe that woman!" Al Terns exclaimed after the trial was over and June Cerf was on her way to serving a sentence of life without parole in the Florida State Women's Prison. "I'd met her a few times before and knew her as being self-centered, but not really a bad person. Not so many fool me that way!"

Paddy had been driving the county van they all went to the courthouse in and had offered Al a lift home. They were in Al's back yard, sitting around the wrought iron table, watching the mullet jumping in the canal.

"She was one ice-cold mama," Marsha agreed. "Her own child, Bill Rinks, or nothing else was going to stand in her way to those millions.

"Want to bet Pickleface wouldn't have lived a year if he'd married her?"

"No takers!" Paddy said. "She knew exactly what she wanted. Little things like people were *not* going to slow her down."

"The little lady was brought up being dirt poor," Ed put in. "She was determined to never be poor again, and took it too far. Much too far."

"Are you defending her now?" Nick asked, incredulous.

"Why, no!" Ed replied, the gleam in his eye. "I believe she should have been executed, but I was not on the jury and I was not the judge."

Nick noted the gleam and dropped out of the debate. He saw the amused look on Al's face, and knew he hadn't missed the fact Ed was baiting the bunch of them.

"You just said it was because of the way she was raised!" Jim accused.

"There's no excuse for *any* woman to turn her back on her own child!" Marsha retorted, hotly. "I think they should fry the bitch in hot oil!"

"The judge tried to be fair," Paddy calmed. "He didn't

have such a vicious crime here."

"Have a Collins, now, Nick?" Al asked, holding up a glass.

"Don't mind if I do!"

Book Two
Odd Jobs

The Job

Lonnie Micks finished the Moorea bed, went to his truck, got two five gallon plastic buckets of mulch, and spread it among the specimen plants, evening it out carefully.

He next spent about an hour placing the petunias in a neat zigzagged color pattern all the way around the bed, then separated the liriope and bordered the entire kidney shape.

Billy, the paperboy, rode by on his Schwinn, called and waved. Lonnie waved back.

Now mulch among all that, then the white marble birdbath in the center of the bed and voila'!

The Shanks drove by in their station wagon. Mrs. Shank was driving, and tooted at him. He waved. He'd be at their place for the afternoon.

Was Mrs. "Oh, now, Lonnie! *You* call me Susan!" Shank really flirting with him, or was she just being nice? She was sort of good looking, but he could never be sure.

No married women! That was a rule he wouldn't break. Gloria and Irene weren't married, but he was getting a bit nervous about Gloria, because she was working around to having him supply her blooms for her florist shop. He didn't pick his flowers. He wanted them on the plant where they belonged.

The birdbath, he'd been against, but Mrs. Parks liked that kind of stuff, so he'd found a way to use it.

He was good at this! Everyone in the neighborhood knew that Lonnie Micks had a talent for designing landscapes and about the greenest thumb in southwest Florida!

He'd taken other places like this, where nobody had ever been able to entice any plants out of the ground, and turned them into showplaces. It was generally a matter of getting the sodium compounds that had coated individual sand particles dissolved and leached through, then in planting things that didn't mind the poor soil. He mixed in a lot of local peat moss with dried bone meal and a bit of chicken manure, then mulched so it wouldn't dry out too fast.

Jill, the teller at the bank, drove by and waved. *She* really was flirting, and no question about it. She was always telling him how his great buns showed off in his tight jeans.

She was all right. A lot of fun, and she wasn't married. Maybe he would.

Lonnie read in some magazine where the average man thinks of sex every so many seconds – or minutes – or something such. It had seemed extreme at the time, but he was doing it right now!

The next bed was under the big laurel oak, so he'd experiment. He grew a lot of things in his back yard people would go "oooh!" and "aaaah!" over. He had a nice surplus of Phaius grandifolius, or Nun's Orchids, and the Parks had the money to pay for the special rich mix he needed.

He carried a wheelbarrow load of plants from his truck. That Walters guy drove by and sort of stared at him. The guy gave him the creeps, sometimes. It wouldn't do any good to wave, because Walters would stare right through him.

Maybe Walters was gay – but wouldn't he be eager to get a wave or something in response, then?

Lonnie had several gay friends. He didn't much care about what anyone did in privacy. He didn't have to join them, but it was embarrassing sometimes when they'd tease him about going around out there with no shirt and shoes and being what they called an "Earth God" type.

He wondered what it would be like, sometimes, a little. What little experience he had with that was when he was only fourteen or fifteen and was a lot more scared than anything else, so he didn't really remember much. It felt good, but sex always did.

Sex again! If he ever wanted any of that kind of thing it was very plainly available. The fact he didn't ever take any of them up on their propositions showed how interested he really was.

He unloaded the wheelbarrow and went back to his truck for another load. An electrician's truck pulled into the drive across the street and Jon got out and waved at him. He smiled and waved back.

Jon *was* gay.

He took the plants to the tree and got a load of mix into the wheelbarrow. Jon came over to ask him if he'd seen Mrs. Lefkowicz go out with anyone. She'd called him the day before to ask him to check out the sockets in her bedroom because they made a sizzling whirring noise, but she didn't seem to be home. Her car was still there.

Lonnie told him he hadn't seen her. Jon said that gave him at least an hour or so of free time and Lonnie drove him totally crazy lifting that heavy stuff and sweating just enough to glisten in the sun.

Lonnie grinned at him and told him to suffer. It was all in fun. Jon was really a nice person, but that kind of joking shouldn't be going on while they were both supposed to be working.

Jon went back to his truck and Lonnie took the mix to start the new bed under the big water oak. Laurel oak. It was a *laurel* oak tree. A water oak was a big *lauarel* oak.

Around the thick trunk of the tree wentthe Mexican orchids. They'd cover the area pretty fast, and the nine months of bright orange flowers started before the Nun's Orchids, so would background the white, purple and brown perfectly.

He was damned good at this! Maybe he could talk the Parks into putting a few large moth orchids on the tree, in coconut husks, so they could be taken in when it was cold.

Now! Around to the back for another of his specialties. He'd plant basil, broccoli, carrots, cabbage, peas and several other vegetables among the beds. A lot of his customers liked that in the back because the vegetables were attractive plants as well as useful in the kitchen.

Mrs. Norton, from the English Manor style house with an adjoining backyard, came to call over the hedge to him and ask some advice on her tea roses. They had scale and were getting some yellowing on their leaves. He told her how he mixed his scale spray with Malathion and dish detergent and to put a little iron and manganese mixed with blood meal around them and sort of dig it in. Lonnie didn't mind giving people free advice, even people like Mrs. Norton, who weren't his customers. He was always practical. She was home all the time and really did like gardening, so why should she pay him or anyone else to do it?

He picked up a few scraps of paper and a piece of cloth and tossed it into his wheelbarrow. It wasn't like the Parks to have anything like that in their lawn or beds, but maybe it had blown in right there. He considered it another one of his little odd jobs to pick up that kind of stuff.

He went back to his old truck to get the seedlings and the tools. He'd already turned the beds Wednesday and treated them for the excess sodium buildup, now he'd have to dig in the organic mix and plant the seedlings.

Jon waved and shrugged. He was just getting into his truck. He backed out of the drive and drove off as Lonnie loaded the trays of plants into the wheelbarrow on top of the mix.

When he was in the backyard, Lonnie carefully laid out the supplies, then poured the mix from the wheelbarrow onto the bed, then went back to get more mix. Put on eight inches of mix and dig it in maybe eighteen inches and you could grow anything.

On the first trip he saw that sexy blond girl from the next block go jogging by. She waved and smiled, but he waved and went on back. She was 'way too young, but she had the look of someone who knew all about it.

Ha! Sex again!

Next trip, Walters went by with his fish-eyed stare. Lonnie ignored him.

Next trip, Billy was coming by and stopped to ask him what to do about an older woman who kept trying to get him to go inside her house when he went there to collect for the paper.

Billy was twelve, which was a little young, so Lonnie told him to say that the paper didn't allow the delivery boys to go inside of anybody's house and neither did his parents, so please don't ask him because it was embarrassing to have to say no.

Lonnie wondered which woman it was who was trying to get a twelve year old kid inside. He could probably guess to within a couple! He shook his head and wondered why anyone would get sexed up over a little kid.

Sex again! The damned magazine had been right!

Last trip, there was no one at all on the street.

Lonnie spread the rich bed mix evenly and began to turn it in. He'd gone only a few feet when the shovel hit something. He'd turned that bed Wednesday, so knew very well there wasn't anything there.

He reached down and pulled out the corner of a black plastic garbage bag. He shook his head, wondering why people like the Parks, who had twice-weekly garbage pickup, would bury anything in the back yard.

Part of his odd jobs! He'd throw it on the truck and haul it off. He would never mention it, because that wouldn't be politic, at all! People like the Parks would get mad as hell if he were to let anyone know they buried garbage in the yard.

Some people burned porno magazines or buried booze bottles, thinking that no one would know they used the stuff.

He grabbed the corner of the bag and yanked. It tore off in his hand.

Great god! Was that a human *foot*!?!

"That was really a nice wedding," Sgt. Marsha Blevins, aide and secretary to Capt. James "Paddy" James (and real power in the office), announced. "Jim and Eileen are going to be a perfect couple for us to compare to."

"It really was nice," Paddy agreed. "Nick, when you and Janet get married, we'll have another party and he can take over your shift for your honeymoon.

"For our night shift man, you spend a lot of days here."

"Oh, well, that's life," Det. Lt. Nathaniel "Nick" Storie replied. "Pat ran off and married the politician's daughter and didn't even bother to invite any of us low-class slobs he worked with."

"He's running for the senate," Sgt. Ed Goins, the new head of the "graveyard" shift homicide cop said. "We must expect him to act like a politician, which merely means he didn't see any way our inclusion could advance his career. The sad truth is that he'll probably win. The way people are fed up with Washington after all their scandals and total inability to deal with reality, people will vote for anyone not there now."

"He's as bad as the worst of them!" Paddy snorted. "I know I won't vote for him. He invited Kathy and me, but Kathy said she had a previous engagement. We went up to Miritello's for dinner."

They were discussing the Wednesday wedding of Jim Hill, day shift homicide and the graveyard shift homicide cop Ed was replacing. Nick was the regular night shift. Jim would have a two week vacation and honeymoon leave, so Nick would take the day shift for him.

"Who's taking my regular shift for the next two weeks?" Nick asked.

Paddy, who was head of the violent crimes operation, answered, "Bill Jenks. It's a slow time of the year, so he can handle it. I'll put Ellen Vickers on with him. She's coming along very well, and needs the experience. We're all here if they get in over their heads."

Sgt. Shirley Kiser, the receptionist, waved for someone to pick up the phone. They'd all heard the attention buzzer sound and had seen the flashing attention light, but had been deliberately ignoring it. Paddy picked it up, and said, "Homicide. James."

There was a short pause, then, "One moment. I'll turn this over to Sgt. Blevins." He handed her the phone. She spoke for a moment, rapidly writing all the while. The others started paying close attention when she said, "Mr. Micks, are you absolutely sure it's a human body? ... A whole human foot is visible?"

She handed Nick a note. He saluted and headed for his car. Ed said he'd ride along, seeing he was there anyhow.

"What is it?" Ed asked, when they got in the car.

"Gardener found a body buried in a fresh vegetable plot in somebody's back yard or something. Those things are usually simple enough cases. Husband kills wife or wife kills husband and buries the body in the new rose bed. These are almost always open and shut cases. Marsh'll send Tiny (Anthony "Tiny" Menthorne, medical examiner) and the lab truck out, but we'll probably have it sewn up before they ever get there."

He checked his map at the corner of Idlewild and Ficus Lane, turned right on Ficus Lane, went to the second block and turned right again.

"Forty seven nineteen Floralee. Right there where the pickup truck is," Nick said. "Vegetable garden should be around back."

He parked and they strolled around the house, admiring

the health and design of the plantings. He could see the neat annual bed in front with the birdbath was recently planted, as was the bed of lush tropicals under a large water oak. There was a weeping elm in a round bed by the front door, with huge white spathiplyllums surrounded by bright amaryllis, driftwood on the stone wall to the left of that, with colorful bromeliads attached and a row of *Aechmeas* in a narrow bed under it.

An extraordinarily handsome man in his early twenties saw them and came to meet them. Nick saw something innocent and likeable about him, an open friendliness that was immediately sensed. It was what they called "charisma" a few years ago. An older man and woman were standing back, gawking at a freshly dug bed with a rich top coating of soil mix spread over most of it. Nick presented his ID, then introduced himself and Ed.

"I'm Lonnie Micks. I found the body when I was digging the bed,. It's a bed I turned on Wednesday, so I can say the body definitely wasn't there then. Definitely."

"Do you recognize the body?" Nick asked.

"I only saw the foot when I tore the bag open and called you. I didn't move anything else. Mr. and Mrs. Parks were in the house. He hadn't gone to his office yet."

Ed had gone to look into the small hole in the bed. He called, "It's in a black polyethylene bag or sheet. I can see what seems to be a woman's foot and ankle and a bit of the calf."

"It's a garbage bag. I pulled the corner up trying to lift it out and it tore open."

"The crime lab will be here in a few minutes, so they'll do whatever else they have to do. It would be better if we stayed back until after they search the area. You found the body, so I'll take your statement.

"Ed, if you don't mind, will you take a statement from

the other two?"

"That's Mr. and Mrs. Parks," Lonnie said. "This is their place."

"I'll take your primary statements," Ed agreed, and led them away from the bed. Nick turned to concentrate on Lonnie Micks again and again the effect was there. Lonnie had a strong impact on him. He looked like one of those ancient Greek statues, or maybe one of those generated ads with a person who was too perfect to be real. He looked, somehow, very clean. There was a perceived air of openness and honesty about him.

Odd.

Nick would estimate twenty two.

Lonnie was dressed only in a pair of faded blue jeans, torn (rather than cut) off just above the ankles. He was slender, but very powerfully built, and was darkly tanned. His hair was thick and moderately long. It was a golden brown. He had clear hazel eyes. His features were fine and almost classic. There was something about him, even under the circumstances, that said he had a keen sense of humor, and that he was above average intelligence. He was extraordinarily handsome, in an innocent, natural sort of way.

"You say you dug the bed Wednesday?"

"Yeah. I turn the soil over and take out all the rocks and stuff, then treat it with special chemicals to dissolve the excess sodium. None of the soil around here will take water. It wants to bead up because of the sodium, so a friend of mine who works for a big chemical company makes me some stuff that takes it off. I dig, screen, and treat the soil for three days before I add the humus and plant."

"The chemicals you use don't hurt the plants?"

"No. It's mostly phosphoric acid and something that acts

like a catalyst, so it forms TSP."

"Which means?"

"It turns it into fertilizer," Lonnie said, with a grin that showed his perfect teeth. "It's not polluting unless you use it right against a creek or something. I wouldn't do that."

"Okay. You say you treated the spot on Wednesday. You worked in front this morning – or is that your work out there?"

"I made the moorea bed there and the orchid bed by the tree. I did that first because it didn't take too much time. Starting from scratch, like I have to in back, takes several hours the first time."

"First time?"

"You can just turn in more humus every year after the first time."

"I see. Have you seen anyone hanging around the area? Speak to anyone? Hear anything suspicious?"

"Well, I talked to the paper boy. His name's Billy. Some woman's trying to get him inside her house and he didn't know what to do about it."

"I'd think most kids would be curious as hell," Nick said, and grinned.

"He's only twelve! Jon was over across the street, but no one was home there, so he chatted a few minutes and left."

"Jon?"

"Yeah. Jon Le Bonne. He has an electrical contracting business. Mrs. Lefkowicz called him yesterday about her lights and said she'd be there, but she wasn't home, so he went back to the super market construction job he's got a contract for.

"I didn't talk to anyone else except Mrs. Norton. About scale on her roses."

"Mrs. Norton?"

"Across the back. The hedge back there is on the property line. The Parks take care of this side and she takes care of her side. Lots of the neighbors here do that kind of plant sharing. Hedges and even flower beds.

"She called me to ask what to do for scale."

"Then she can see across the hedge?"

"On the part toward the lower end. It's only four feet high there. Between the houses, it's eight feet – for privacy, you know. These are big lots out here. A little over an acre each, so they put up fences and hedges where it'll stop anyone from looking directly into their houses."

"Did you see anyone else? Anyone you didn't talk to?"

"Just the people driving by. The Shanks, the Walters creep, Jill – she works at the bank in Bodkins Street Mall. I waved at them all – except Walters."

"Why do you say he's a creep?"

"He just *is*!" Lonnie replied, matter-of-factly. "If you wave or say anything, he stares right through you. It could only be me he's that way with. Everybody else around here is always friendly. He's just, I don't know ... a *creep*!"

"Rich?"

"Well, yes. It's sorta upscale in the whole area, but no more than anyone else. Why?"

"I was thinking it might be like the golf courses over near my place. No one's allowed to work in anyone's yard without shoes and a shirt. It's stupid, but you meet all kinds as a cop."

"I don't see how anyone can work with all those clothes in the sun in southwest Florida. Nobody's ever said anything about that to me. Not to get me to put any clothes *on*!"

Nick grinned. "They try to get you to take them off?"

Lonnie blushed. "Well, I guess it's just that so many women are home alone all day and their husbands are ... that isn't what I mean!" He was fiery red.

Nick laughed. "I get them asking me if I'd like to come in for a cold beer on such a hot day, sometimes."

"Oh, I don't mind that. I mean, I don't mess with married women. It's a rule."

Tiny and the crime lab van pulled up and parked out front. Tiny waved and heaved himself out of the van. He stood six five and weighed over three hundred pounds, thus the nickname.

Paddy stood six three and weighed two thirty five. Nick was always a little awed when the two mountainous men were in the same room.

"Who, where, what?" Tiny demanded, wiping sweat off his broad forehead with a white towel he carried for that purpose. "The damned forensics van's *hot*!"

"Don't know," Nick replied. "Looks like a woman's foot. In that bed over there. We thought we'd wait and let you dig it up."

"One of my perks. I'm the boss. I don't dig shoveling."

"Buried? Deep?"

"Not deep," Nick said. "In a garbage bag."

Tiny yelled for his crew to bring a gurney and shovels and the kit.

"Frog" Forest slung several cameras around his body and slogged toward the burial scene, using a camcorder as he went. He stopped to pan the landscape, and said, "Damn nice work.

"Over by where Ed's pointing? Maybe I should pretend to not see 'im."

"OK. Comb the whole area. There could be something overlooked," Tiny agreed. "If the victim's not the wife, we'll need some answers. A cigarette butt used by the only person in the whole damned US who smokes that brand would be nice, for a change."

"I found some paper scraps and stuff earlier over by the

property line hedge," Lonnie said. "I threw it into the junkbox on my truck."

"Show it to me!" Nick demanded. "This place, you could eat off of! Any papers could be important."

Lonnie grinned and led Nick out to the truck, with Tiny panting along. There was a small cardboard box up by the cab with a flap that opened back. Lonnie lifted it out and handed it to Tiny, who opened it and asked, "Which is from here?"

"That piece of brownish-white cloth and the two scraps from a telephone pad. That little foil wrapper and plastic piece. That white tissue."

"That it? You sure it all came from here?" Tiny asked, picking each piece out carefully with the tongs he carried in his pocket to drop them into individual baggies.

"That's all. It was sort of together over by the hedge on that end (pointing to the lower end)."

"Show me as close to exactly where you found it as you can," Nick said, as Frog yelled to Tiny he had all the prelim pictures they'd need.

Tiny grunted and headed for the bed where the body was buried while Lonnie led Nick to a point where the hedge went from four to eight feet.

"That hedge is really thick!" Nick said. "How do you keep it so full?"

"It's all pittosphorum along here, so it trims easy. I use a lot of lime stuff on it. It gets really thick in alkaline soil or tall in more acid.

"The stuff was right along there, close to the pass."

"Pass?" Nick looked to see a narrow angled slot that was cut to pass through the hedge.

"The Parks and the Nortons are good friends, so they have a pass through the hedge. I cut it at a long angle so the hedge looks solid from either side until you get right up to it. Always make hedge passes out in the full sun. If you have too much shade the leaves won't fill inside the cut.

"I guess you don't care about that. Shop talk."

"I do. I'm getting married before too long and I like to keep my place neat. So, as close as you can tell, where was each item?"

"It was all right along here spread out about three feet almost under the hedge."

Nick carefully checked the entrance to the slot, then went in and along the short cut. There was a small piece of white plastic inside, hung on a cut-off piece of limb. He yelled for Tiny, just as a woman came into the slot from the other side. She was what the English would call "solid" to the point Nick thought of her as one of the type in a lot of the old English detective movies. She was even dressed in a khaki outfit with a pith helmet!

"Who are all you people? Whatever is going on over here? Lonnie! What's happened? Is it Melvin's heart? What are all these people doing here?"

"I'm afraid I found a body when I was turning over the vegetable patch. It wasn't there last Wednesday.

"Mrs. Norton, Lt. Storie."

"What kind of body?" she asked, with a blank look.

"It seems to be a woman's body," Nick replied, gently. "The coroner's men are getting it out of the flower bed so we can get a look at it.

"Have you noticed any unusual – or I should say, any activity over here since Wednesday?"

"A woman's body? Here? Buried in a vegetable bed? Whatever are you blathering about? This isn't some slum tract, officer! That kind of thing does *not* happen here. There must be some mistake."

"I'm afraid it can – does – happen almost everywhere.

The difference seems to be that murders in the higher class areas are generally planned and executed more carefully. There generally isn't the publicity drug or gang killings tend to generate, because they generally aren't so violent and sudden.

"Have you noticed any unusual or odd activity over here since Wednesday?"

"No. I wouldn't, over there. The hedge isn't low enough and I haven't been home until late at night. I...."

"You stopped? Have you thought of something?"

"Well, yes and no. I may be quite wrong, but, as I drove in last night, I could have sworn somebody was by the pass. Right there. The car's lights sweep across there whenever I turn into the drive, so it was only a vague sort of impression. It could have simply been a shadow."

"What time?" Nick asked, as Tiny came up. Mrs. Norton stared in awe at the huge man.

"Er, oh! Let's see then," she said, tearing her eyes off of Tiny. "I left the meeting at eleven thirty, then stopped at Jen's place – that's Jennie Leigh – for about fifteen minutes when I drove her home, then stopped at Kash 'N Karry for some things. It was between twelve thirty and one. Pretty close to ... it was exactly five to one! I listen to the classic hour on Quality Radio, and they broke for the news precisely as I turned off the motor. Five to one. Exactly!"

"That could be more important than we could possibly guess, at this point. Thank you, Mrs. Norton."

"Tiny, get this and see what it is, will you?" He showed Tiny the plastic scrap. Tiny yelled for Frog.

"Frog?" Mrs. Norton asked.

"Yes. He's the forensics cameraman," Nick answered. "It's only his nickname, not a physical feature."

Frog came over, took some camcorder shots of the

plastic bit, then several stills, then sort of wandered away after Nick showed him where the scraps had been found. He photographed the whole area.

"I'll bet he's lots of fun," Lonnie said.

"Frog? You're kidding!" Tiny replied, slipping the little piece of plastic into a baggie. "He seems to be in some other world, most of the time."

"He's putting you on." Lonnie grinned. "He's just acting like a sixties hippie because you fall for it. I bet he's really good at his job, too!"

"The best," Nick agreed. "I've always said he acts like he does because that's the way he sees crime photographers on the TV. He doesn't want to disappoint his public." He and Lonnie laughed, and Tiny nodded agreement.

"Lieutenant!" Mrs. Norton demanded, in an exasperated tone, "Are you supposed to be investigating a violent death here or chatting about people?"

"You relax and you remember things," Tiny told her. "It's Nick's favorite technique. Talk about anything but the crime and things will pop into your mind. Concentrate, and it's mostly a blank.

"They're ready to lift the body out. Think anyone can ident it?"

"I probably could. If she's anybody from the neighborhood, I'll probably know her. I don't want to look at her, Nick, but you can't ask the Parks or Mrs. Norton to."

"What?" Mrs. Norton said. "I was an emergency ward nurse for twenty-odd years! Bodies don't bother me!"

She marched (literally) over to the bed followed by Nick and Lonnie with Tiny bringing up the rear. She looked at the garbage bag laying there with the foot sticking out, then at the Parks and Ed standing fifty feet off by the back door to the house.

"Gina, take Melvin inside! Now! This isn't the kind of

thing you should be gawking at!" she turned to the two men with the shovels, who were staring at her like she was crazy.

"Open it!" she demanded.

Frog let out a sharp little explosive laugh and quickly focused his camcorder on the scene. Tiny shook his head and shrugged, then waved for the men to move back. He slipped on surgical gloves, took out a scissors knife, and carefully split the bag lengthwise, then folded it open to expose the nude body of a woman in her mid-thirties, slightly plump, and about five seven.

"Hmm. I'll be thoroughly damned!" Mrs. Norton said, studying the scene carefully. "It's Jeannie Lefkowicz. From across the street there. She was strangled. Marks on the throat. Bruise over her left eye and her nose bled a little. Bruise high on the left biceps. Lips are bruised and cut a little. No particular evidence of rape, but that'll have to be checked."

She picked up a hand and dropped it.

"Been dead eight to ten hours. Maybe twelve, but I don't think so. The bag would conserve some heat, but rigor's about right for eight to ten.

"If you've got all the pictures you need, young man, you can turn her over so I can check lividity and marks."

"*If* you don't object too terribly, I think that's my job!" Tiny said, hotly.

"Well then do it! I last saw Jeannie, umm, yesterday morning around, oh ... nine thirty, when I went to market. I stopped to tell her about the meeting to stop the incinerator and she said she wasn't getting involved. Too many like that!"

"Everyone on this block and both the blocks east and west use this street to come and go," Lonnie said. "It's easier than fighting the four-way stops every corner on the others.

"It's Mrs. Lefkowicz, so that's why she wasn't home when Jon stopped. He thought she would be there because she called him."

"Did she live alone?" Nick asked.

"Josef, her husband, owns a fleet of over the road trucks. He drives one of them himself. He's gone three or four days at the time. He's been out on his run to Atlanta since yesterday morning. Jeannie told me about that when I talked to her. He won't be back until the day after tomorrow."

"We'll let the lab crew handle the rest of this," Nick said. "Ed, we'll get the names and addresses of anyone who might know anything, then we'll canvas the neighborhood. If you'll start next door to the north I'll finish with Mrs. Norton and start to the south. We'll work around to the west and come back down the block over there to Mrs. Norton's house. We'll take the block behind the Lefkowicz place after that.

"Tiny, can you get the information to Paddy to try to find Josef Lefkowicz, en route to Atlanta?

"Mrs. Norton, would you know the name of Mr. Lefkowicz's company?"

"Lefkowicz Trucking. The office is over off of Airport Road. I think the better way to contact him quickly would be through their own call system."

"What's that?"

"The dispatcher calls along the route with his hi-frequency radio to contact him and have him call back for emergency messages. They use their citizens' band radios in whatever area he's supposed to be in.

"His radio name, what I believe they call his handle, is `Hell Hauler.'"

The woman was amazing.

Tiny nodded, and bent over to study the body closely. Nick sighed and said he'd better start with the Parks if Mrs. Norton didn't have anything else at that time. He already had Lonnie's statement and would get back to him if anything new came up.

"Mr. Parks, I know this kind of thing can be awfully hard on people, but we'll have to find out everything we can as quickly as we can to prevent it happening again. If you don't know, yet, the body is that of your neighbor across the street, Jeannie Lefkowicz. We can't think of any reason she would be buried in your back garden, except that the bed was freshly dug, so digging again would possibly not be noticed.

"We'll have to know everyone who knew it was being prepared, but that could well be coincidence. The killer might have come across the yard at random and would have seen it, but we don't think so."

"The killer would have come across at night if it was random: therefore, it was someone who came across during the day," Mr. Parks agreed. "I don't have any idea who it could be. There's been no one here, except Lonnie since the bed was begun that I'm aware of, but I'm generally gone after ten thirty until perhaps five or five thirty. I have a general insurance agency. I'm there from eleven until five Monday through Friday."

"I've not had any visitors except for the people from Elise's group," Mrs. Parks answered. "People sometimes stop to talk to Lonnie and walk in. I don't see many of them, because I go out a lot.

"I wasn't here on Wednesday while he was working, so I don't know. Lonnie's very popular here. He's easily the best gardener anyone ever had and the younger women are all so very much interested.

"Isn't he the most handsome man you ever saw? And he's very intelligent, too! And talented! He designs every-thing!"

"Gina, I do think you have a crush on the gardener!" Melvin chided, with an indulgent smile.

She blushed. "Well, I certainly think a single woman could do far worse! I know I'd certainly introduce Carole Jean to him if she wasn't already married!

"Carole's our daughter, Lieutenant Storie. I'm prattling on about things, so I won't have to think about Jeannie. I didn't much care for her or her husband, but I've never wished her any harm."

"You didn't like her?"

"I didn't *dis*like her, but I didn't care to ever socialize with them. I'm afraid I tend toward a certain bigotry. They really didn't have many of the social graces I'm accus-tomed to."

"Er, Gina's a bit of a snob, at times, but I am, too," Melvin interjected. "The truth being, they tended to be a bit ... vulgar. She didn't dress appropriately for the neighborhood and he would sometimes walk around the lawn drinking beer from the can. We were raised with the custom of dressing properly at all times and of not drinking outside the den or dining room."

"Yet Lonnie can work around your lawn with no shirt?" Nick asked.

"Of course. Lonnie's a gardener, not a resident," Gina said, with a bit of a smile. "We did admit that we're snobs. The simple fact being, Lonnie is a very pleasant person to look at partially unclothed. Jeannie wasn't and Josef isn't. We're quite willing to bend the rules if the incentive is great enough. We get Lonnie as he is or we don't get him at all. I don't have the skills of Elise, so our lawn would look like the Lefkowicz's if we didn't have him to handle things, so we use a different standard for residents than for workers.

"Our snobbery would be thrown into crisis if Lonnie were to move next door. Then we'd be forced to change those rules for the residents or all us silly women would lose the chance to look at such a beautiful person in a natural setting. I think we'd feel rather differently if he were a plumber or something. The setting is half of it. Lonnie's a natural thing among the plants.

"I can tell you this because Melvin knows it. We girls picture Lonnie in a primeval forest among the trees wearing what we feel is natural for someone like him. Nothing. Lonnie's our own private Pan."

"He's considered a satyr, then?" Nick asked, with another of his ever-present grins. "I have to know if either of you saw or heard anything last night after about ten o'clock until around one this morning."

"We came home around twelve thirty," Melvin said. "We were at the Barbara B. Mann Theater up in Ft. Myers. Beverly Sills and the opera. Excellent performance!

"We came home and went to bed. I've had bypass surgery and the doctors raise hell about me being up after eleven, but we really do enjoy the arts."

"Then you saw and heard nothing?"

"Nothing," Gina repeated, and Melvin nodded.

"The people who you said came over with Mrs. Norton's group? What group, and do you know them?"

"It was one of her civic causes," Gina answered. "Stop the incinerator or stop the food irradiating or stop nuclear power or something. I do always try to be civil to them, but I don't remember very much about it, except wishing she'd take that sort of thing elsewhere."

"I'll ask her about it, then. Thank you. I'm sorry about all the inconvenience, but what can you do?"

Ed was waiting in front of the Norton house when Nick got there. Neither had found anything pertinent, except Ed said the people next door, the Youngs, thought they saw a pale light through the hedge about midnight, but couldn't be too sure because the hedge was so thick there. Elise Norton saw them standing there and came to ask what they'd learned.

"Not very much, M'am, I'm afraid," Ed said. "It appears the killer was quite skilled at not making much noise."

"I have a couple more questions for you, now," Nick said. "That bed wasn't even started until Wednesday, so the killer was someone who was around to see it between then and last evening. Mrs. Parks said only Lonnie and a group you brought over had seen it, unless someone came back to talk to Lonnie on Wednesday while he was working on the bed. What I have to know...."

"Is who, besides myself, was there. I know perfectly well the killer had to have been there since the bed was dug on Wednesday. I'm not stupid. He or she also had to know about the pass. I saw the killer when I drove in, assuming I'm telling the truth and am not, myself, the murderer.

"If I hadn't been at that meeting and hadn't taken Jennie home I would be a complete fool to tell you I was and did: therefore, only the people in my group, the Parks, Lonnie or someone who came back there to speak with Lonnie would know.

"The Parks are worse than ludicrous as viable suspects, and my own alibi is unshakable, because I was at the meeting and I did take Jennie home, so wouldn't have the time.

"The killer is someone from my group or someone Lonnie talked to back there Wednesday.

"We were circulating a petition to curtail the obscene tax increases every year and about the planned incinerator that will pollute miles away. There were nine people in the group, besides myself. The Youngs and Jennie were at the meeting with me, so they're out.

"Susan and Tim Shank, Jill Finney – she's the teller at the bank and the coordinator for that committee – Victor Walters and Gloria Valdez, who owns the florist shop.

"Susan Shank is a typical housewife and Tim owns an exclusive men's clothing store in North Naples. Victor Walters is a free-lance photographer who produces a number of those educational shows for PBS.

"Jill and Susan are too small to have killed her, carried her across to that spot, and dug the hole, even though the soil had been loosened, so Tim Shank, Victor Walters, Gloria Valdez – who isn't nearly so fragile as she tries to look – and whoever Lonnie comes up with are your suspects."

"Which one did it?"

"I haven't the foggiest idea. I think probably someone Lonnie talked to over there," she answered, after a moment's pause to consider.

"What about Lonnie?"

"Ridiculous! Absolutely not! Lonnie would never kill anyone and bury them like that! If Lonnie killed anyone he'd bury her deeper and plant the flowers over her and no one would ever know – besides which, if our Lonnie did do it you wouldn't ever get a conviction. Not if a woman were on the jury."

"Then I'm glad I don't think he did it," Nick said, with his grin.

"You'd let him off if you were on the jury?"

"Certainly Mr. Storie, I'm quite human and I'm female. If I *saw* him do any such thing I wouldn't believe it. I'd swear I was hallucinating or something.

"I sometimes wonder if there really are aliens from

flying saucers here when I look at him. If there are, he's one!"

"Well, we'd better talk with Lonnie again and head on back to the station. Thanks again.

"If it means anything I think you saw the murderer as you drove in this morning."

She nodded. "That seems inescapable."

Ed and Nick went to Nick's car and started for the station.

Ed asked, "Why do you think she saw the murderer?"

"Several reasons. The Mrs. Nortons of this world do not ever imagine things. She very definitely saw someone by the pass through the hedge. The Parks had just come home from the opera, so the killer had stopped digging the hole or something and stepped through the pass to wait for them to get to bed. Mrs. Norton drove up and he slipped back to the Parks' side of the hedge."

"I tend to agree. Lonnie is working at the Bloch house. It's at nineteen oh seven Hotchkis. Three blocks down on the next street. You were planning to ask him about visitors on Wednesday."

Nick turned down Iris to Hotchkis. He was getting a street plan firmly in mind because he was going to have to figure the route of the killer, sooner or later.

Only Tim Shank had come back to talk to him about making a rock garden by the pool.

Nick was introduced to Karen Bloch, a seventeen year old girl who was already a striking beauty and who seemed quite a bit too knowledgeable about sex – and who obviously adored Lonnie (Who seemed embarrassed by it). Her mother, Lilith, stated she didn't know what the youth of today was coming to, but she was damned glad Lonnie had such a level head and she knew she could trust him totally. It was plain enough mama wouldn't disapprove if maybe Lonnie and Karen found a mutual interest. She said any woman in the whole world would want a man (stressed) like Lonnie for their daughter. Ed remarked on the way back to the station that the lady seemed somewhat disappointed in her own husband's performance.

"How do you figure?"

"She was comparing what she thought Lonnie would be like to what she knew her husband was like. I can't help but believe sex is somehow behind this whole thing. Women can't help but think about sex when they look at that one!"

"I can trust Mrs. Norton's diagnosis of Mrs. Lefkowicz. I've seen rape-murder victims enough that I don't think she was raped."

"Rape isn't about sex. There's far too much about sex in this case and it all seems to revolve around sexy Lonnie, somehow."

"Maybe you're right. Personally speaking, I don't think he has anything to do with it, except for finding her body."

"Maybe. I don't think he had anything to do with it that he knows about, but I think something to do with him is why there was a murder. Maybe a woman who found he was getting too friendly with her wanted to reduce the competition a little. Better the odds, so to speak."

"No. Then she would never have buried Mrs. Lefkowicz where Lonnie was sure to find her. I wonder about that! What if the body was left there specifically so he'd find it?"

"I don't get it?" Ed asked, watching Nick carefully.

"I don't know. Maybe the killer thought Lonnie would simply bury her deeper and plant the flowers over her."

"And?"

"We'd get a report of a body buried under a flowerbed at the Parks that only Lonnie could possibly have put there."

"It doesn't seem at all logical."

"I know. Nothing else does, either. I think I'm going to be looking very carefully for a certain odd little innuendo. If I get it, I'll have the killer.

"We need a motive. I hope it's not a nut case."

"Innuendo? Whatever do you mean?" Ed asked as they turned into the parking lot at the station.

"It's more a matter of ... Lonnie told me no married women. It's a rule. Lonnie doesn't ever break his rules of conduct. He never had anything like that going with Mrs. Lefkowicz.

"What if he was supposed to find the body and hide it?

"He didn't, so the killer can't push murder off on him.

"Next step, make it look like Lonnie was having an affair with her and he'd suddenly become our prime suspect again."

He turned off the ignition.

"Here's Tiny's updated spot report on what we have so far," Paddy announced, dropping the file on Nick's desk next morning. "We located Josef Lefkowicz and he's on his way home. It's important to get inside the house. I've had it watched to prevent any interference, but the murder probably took place there. You can find a key in the tray under the pot of geraniums by the door, according to Mr. Lefkowicz.

"There's another little case, so I'm pulling Ed and putting him on it. You should be able to handle this one, now."

"I'm putting a chronological chart together," Nick replied. "My big problem is motive. This kind of thing can take a lot of time, I'm afraid. We really have nothing to hang anything on."

Paddy shrugged and told Marsha to call Ed to come in to handle the Evans case. He was going to have to be in court for the full day and probably most of the next. Tiny wouldn't be available, either. Dr. David Klein would be in charge of the forensics team and was acting ME until Tiny was again released back to duty.

Nick opened the file to read that, much as Elise Norton had deduced, Mrs. Lefkowicz was probably attacked suddenly, struck in the face and on the head, then was strangled. She wasn't raped. The struggle was most probably a short one.

Next was the small piece of plastic from the pass in the hedge. It was thin polyethylene, the same constitution and thickness as grocery sacks. A bit of red printing on a minute piece confirmed that's what it was.

The telephone messages were from a standard sticky pad and were badly deteriorated and undecipherable. They'd been written in water-soluble ink that had faded to nothing in the before-dawn sprinkling of the lawn. There were no prints.

The plastic and foil piece was from a videotape package.

The cloth sample wasn't identified, as of yet, though it was a light fabric much like that used in draperies as a fronting mat. It was a square about five inches by seven. There was some high-calcium dust and some light oil on it.

Someone came through the pass in the hedge carrying a sack of typical stuff from a wastepaper basket. The sack caught on the branch and tore, dumping some of the stuff there. Most of it was probably picked up again, but it was dark and a few bits were overlooked by the base of the hedge. The killer was probably the only one who could have been there, but why was he carrying stuff from a typical wastebasket? What was in that garbage?

Nick didn't have much. Someone who had recently been at the Parks' house had killed Jeannie Lefkowicz and had buried her body in the vegetable bed he'd seen being prepared there. He'd killed her about eleven, then had buried her around one. The Parks had come home before he was through, so he slipped out through the hedge cut to wait until they were retired. Elise Norton saw the killer as she turned into her drive. He'd slipped back through to finish the job of burying the body, tearing his garbage bag in the pass.

Did he panic and bury the body much more shallowly than he'd planned? Was the original idea to bury it deep enough to where Lonnie wouldn't discover it, then the Parks returned home, followed by Mrs. Norton, so he threw some soil over it and got the hell out of there before someone saw him?

Nick could now concentrate on Tim Shank and Victor

Walters, but he didn't have diddly-squat on either of them and knew it. He hadn't interviewed either of them, but Shank's alibi would be Susan, who was probably asleep and wouldn't know if he'd been out. Walters wouldn't have an alibi, living alone.

One thing was certain. If there was anything to know about that neighborhood, Lonnie probably knew it. He wasn't the type to talk, but maybe the seriousness of murder would loosen his tongue, to some extent.

Lonnie would be in that neighborhood. His truck would tell Nick exactly where to find him, so Nick headed toward the Lefkowicz house. The key wasn't exactly where it was supposed to be. It had been dropped on the porch behind the geranium. Nick started to pick it up, but stopped before he touched it. Mrs. Lefkowicz would have her own key to her house. So would Josef – so who had taken that key from under the geranium?

The killer. There would be evidence of the murder in there, because the killer would have used the key to get in.

Was Jeannie Lefkowicz involved in an affair that somehow got out of hand?

Nick got the kit from his car and carefully dusted the key, but there were no prints on it. Either the killer wore gloves, which even the most amateurish ones did anymore, or he had wiped the key carefully.

Nick picked up the key and used it to open the door.

The house was comfortable and "lived-in" neat, which meant it was clean and arranged, but there were the signs of a comfortable home such as magazines on the sofa, a dust cloth left on a table, a shirt thrown across the back of a chair. It smelled slightly of spices and herbs.

Nick moved around to find nothing out of place, except in the bathroom. As he stepped to look through the open door, he noticed some white powder in the center of the door sill. There was a broken cold cream jar on the floor, a puddle of water by the shower door, a spot of blood on the little rug in front of the toilet and the ventilator grille over the door was removed.

Why? That could be vitally important.

The medicine cabinet door was open and was twisted slightly downward on its hinge.

That removed ventilator grille was the thing that caught his eye as being the most important item. It was a piece of ventilation return flow duct between the bathroom and the bedroom and wouldn't even be noticeable if it weren't for that powder in front of the door. That was from the sheetrock the ventilator grille was screwed into, meaning the grille had been yanked out.

The bathroom was almost exactly the color of that piece of cloth Lonnie found in the Parks' back yard. There was some calcium dust on the cloth. Sheetrock dust was calcium dust.

Where was that grille? Why was it taken? Was the cloth over the grille for some reason?

Nick went to his car phone to call the lab. He told them to bring a crew and he'd meet them at the door. He went back inside and through to the kitchen. Everything was normal.

He thought a minute, then went from the kitchen to the garage, found a small four-step ladder, and carried it back to the bathroom, then climbed to look into the opening the grille was removed from. There had been something hidden in that vent space. Something that had been removed. Marks in the thick dust showed that, plainly.

There were also two thin wire couples laying loose inside. They seemed to lead into the wall space to the right.

He picked up the wire and got a small shock. He touched

the ends of the wires together and got a small electric spark and the bathroom light flickered.

So. Something had been in that vent that was turned on – or something such – when the bathroom light was turned on. He would have to locate the electrician Lonnie Micks had mentioned.

He picked up the other wire couple and touched the tips. Nothing.

There was also a small piece cut from the ventilator grille into the bedroom. About two inches square.

He climbed to the top step to look through the hole. He was looking directly at the bed and the side of the bed toward the bathroom. He turned around to see the whole shower end of the bathroom would be visible from the grille on that side.

Nick thought a few seconds, held up the wires, slowly climbed down to turn on the bedroom lights, then climbed back up to touch the wire tips together, getting the spark and a flicker of the bedroom lights.

He climbed down and moved the ladder, then went to sit on the front porch for a few minutes until the lab crew and van arrived. He told them to check out the bathroom carefully, and to note the things he'd noted, particularly to photograph the ventilator and its interior, then he went looking for Lonnie. He had a lot of it, now.

Lonnie was taking some 100# sacks of fertilizer out of his truck. Karen Bloch and two women in their mid twenties were standing there talking to him. Tim and Susan Shank were driving by. They waved and Lonnie waved back.

Actually, the women were watching Lonnie work and making cute comments now and then. Karen seemed jealous that the others were there.

"Hi, Nick!" Lonnie greeted. "Anything yet?"

"Not anything I can talk about. I have to ask you a couple of things."

"Shoot!" Lonnie grinned. "You know Karen. This is Frieda Leven and Hilda Johanssen. They live a couple blocks down that way. Nick Storie."

"We wanted to know the best kind of fertilizer to use on our azaleas," Frieda said. "Our lots run together and we share a big bed of them under the oaks."

"Oh, crap! Talk about *fertilizer*!" Karen mumbled, just audibly, getting hard looks from the two women. "One guess which bed they'd *like* to share!"

"*Child*, shouldn't you be in school or something?" Hilda asked, pointedly. "Don't you have some homework to do?"

"I've finished school! Won't your loving *husbands* be looking for you?"

"Lonnie doesn't do windows or married women," Nick said. "You may be through with school, young lady, but you're not of legal age yet. You're *all* wasting your time."

Frieda laughed, and said, "We do sound like cats don't we? We mostly like to tease Lonnie. He's fun to be around. He doesn't take us seriously and he won't allow us to take ourselves seriously, either.

"I only speak for us adults."

Karen hissed, turned red, and stamped off. Lonnie shook his head. Nick grinned.

Frieda asked if she and Hilda should leave.

"Yes. I'll have to speak with Lonnie about a murder investigation in progress. It's private. It's much more than private, it's confidential in a legal sense."

"Plain enough, Nick!" Hilda said. "Do *you* do married women?"

"Only if I'm the one they're married to." They waved gaily and walked off, giggling together.

"They only come over whenever Karen starts hanging

around," Lonnie explained. "I sort of told Frieda how I didn't want anyone getting the wrong idea, so they come over when she comes. They play a little game, cutting at each other. It's all in fun."

"For you maybe, but they're far more serious than you know. I saw a very real rivalry there."

"Over me? Really?" Lonnie asked. He seemed surprised. "I just never know when they're serious!"

"For your attention. Does Susan Shank play those games with you? Ever?"

"Well, I sometimes think she means it."

"Does Tim know about it?"

"Uh-huh. He told me not to pay any attention to her, because she's teasing, but I could see he doesn't like it. I let him know I never mess with any married women. He said he'd learned that, and he wasn't mad at me, but it sort of grinds on a man for the wife to throw herself at someone else."

"Does Victor Walters get upset about women coming onto you all the time?"

"The creep? Why would he even care? He's not married to any of them," Lonnie answered, confused.

"Could be he's jealous because they don't throw themselves at him like that."

"They don't? You saw how Frieda and Hilda teased you the same way they tease me. I think most women do that with men. It's just the way they are."

"Lonnie, I'm flattered when they do that. It's not that often. With you standing right there, it's sort of a rush. Women don't throw themselves at men very often. They throw themselves at you because, as one woman said, you're their Pan. You're a fantasy."

"*Me*?! I mean, but why would they...?" He blushed deeply. "I know it was Mrs. Norton who told you that. She tells them I should be a satyr out in the woods, put there only for foolish women to dream of. I've read about Pan and the Greek myths. She was probably.... I don't do anything to make them act like that! I like sex and to play and tease as much as anyone else, but I don't *do* anything to make them do that!"

"Lonnie?"

"What?"

"Don't ever change! You're the last of the innocents. I really believe you don't know you're the perfect ideal of a man for a lot of women. Be careful, Lonnie. It's a dangerous game, anymore."

"Nick, I didn't have anything to do with the murder. I don't know anything about it."

"No. I meant things like AIDS. As to the murder, there's some small possibility the body was put there to try to implicate you."

"I do try to be careful about AIDS. Why would anyone want to implicate me?"

"Because they're jealous. Because someone's wife wants you more and them less. Maybe because you're getting it and they're not. You just be careful. I've found something that makes me think we may have a psycho of a sort on our hands."

Lonnie made a helpless gesture and shrugged.

"Lonnie, you told me yesterday that an electrician came to the Lefkowicz house before you found the body? Did he say why he was there?"

"Something about weird noises coming from some wall switches, I think. That was Jon Le Bonne. He's working on a big strip store and supermarket they're building on the corner of forty one and East Gulfbreeze. It's only a couple of blocks over that way. Take Iris and turn right on Lemontree and you run right into it.

"You found something?"

"I think so. I'll drive over there. It's only a quarter to nine. Will he be there?"

"Yeah. He works early."

Nick went to his car, saying he'd be back in a few minutes. He wanted to check out a couple of points.

Jon was wiring a three phase system into a walk-in meat cooler, but was more than willing to chat while he worked.

"Lonnie Micks said you went to the Lefkowicz home yesterday morning?"

"God! That guy drives me wild! "He runs around two-thirds naked and every queen and fish in the state goes out of their mind! He doesn't even *know* it!

"Did you notice that there's no one anywhere on the streets over there, but the block he's working on has women and girls strolling up and down the sidewalks and driving by constantly?

"Christ! Just looking at him drives people nuts!"

"I take it you're gay?" Nick asked, with a grin.

"If I wasn't already, I'd damned well turn queer for him!" Jon returned the grin. "Jeannie called and said the wall switches made odd crackling and humming noises in the bedroom. I told her I'd stop by and check for a short. There's a lot of aluminum wiring in houses built around the time that one went up. It can be dangerous, more or less.

"I'll bet Lonnie was really shocked when he dug her up. I know I'd freak.

"She was nice. Most people in there are.

"Do you have any ideas about who did it?"

"I have a couple I'm checking out. Do you know the Shanks?"

"Tim and Sue? Sure. Tim Shanks wouldn't be having an affair with Jeannie. Sue's the one who plays around while the hubby's out busting his hump to support her. I think probably Tim would kill her before he'd kill anyone else. He does get pissed, sometimes."

"I can see why he would. What about Victor Walters?"

"The weirdo PBS photographer? I don't know him," Jon said, with a distasteful twist of the mouth. "He'd never be caught around any of us damned, in the religious sense, immoral types, particularly gays. His religion tells him we're gay because we chose to be evil immoral devils.

"You ask me, he's queer as a three dollar bill, himself! He just doesn't know it yet!"

"Lonnie doesn't much care for him either."

"Lonnie parades around in public with no shirt! He's bound for the hottest spot in lowest hell and damnation, brethrens and cisterns!"

They talked a few minutes, then Nick went back to Lonnie's job, where he found Lonnie was talking to a young boy. He was introduced to Billy Milton, the paper-boy.

"Lon dug up that woman!" Billy said, eagerly. "Cool!"

"It was definitely *not* cool!" Lonnie said, sharply. "It was scary and more than a little disgusting! Lt. Storie's the homicide policeman who's trying to find who the killer is."

"Wow! Really? Did you ever get in any shootouts?"

"Only once. It's not anything like the TV crap. When people really get shot, they stay shot. They don't wash the makeup off, pick up a big paycheck, and go home to a steak dinner."

"Wow! Did you get shot at?"

"I got hit. Right here on the side of my leg. I was luckier than the one who shot me. He took four shots to the chest."

"Did you shoot him?" Billy asked, awed.

"No. I bled a lot and ended up in the hospital for a week.

As soon as the infection was cured I had to use a wheel-chair for more than a month, then I had to learn to walk again. It still hurts, sometimes.

"Billy, it's not like the movies. I got hurt and two people are dead. There was no glamor to it. It was sordid and sick. I didn't jump up from the hospital bed and chase the crooks, after crashing twenty cars and blowing up a couple of buildings. There were no heroes there. The cops who were involved were sick and ashamed.

"Two men who had held up a grocery store, late one night. They'd stabbed a pregnant woman and shot the man and woman working the cashier's stand. They weren't big deals, they were little petty scumbags with no intelligence. Everybody lost. Everybody was dirtied by it. Now nobody wants to think about it or talk about it."

"Why were the cops ashamed if they shot a couple of robbers who shot at them first?" Billy was clearly con-fused.

"They were ashamed to be members of the human race. People who do the kinds of things those two did make everyone a little less. Everyone becomes a little dirtied by that kind of senseless thing. They were mainly ashamed because they're even necessary in our society. They were ashamed because they had failed."

"But why?" Billy asked, looking to Lonnie.

"Why had we failed? Because we weren't able to stop them before they stabbed one woman and shot another two other people. The cops were frustrated and ashamed because they were only human and those two had made being human less than it was before."

"Nobody can stop it," Billy argued. "Everybody knows that."

"That's exactly right. Do you see?"

Billy thought a minute, then said, "No."

"It's the race diminishment theory," Lonnie explained. "Anything one person does affects everyone else, because we're all part of the same thing. If you do something positive, you make the whole race grow. If you do something negative, you diminish the whole race.

"Look at it like this. There's this UFO studying Earth and the people on this planet to determine if we're good enough to join the galactic society. He reads a paper, watches a TV show and scans a big city with a telescope. He has only twenty four hours to make his decision about what happens to humanity.

"The newspapers tell about a bunch of violent rapes, murders and robberies. The TV news is about our crooked politicians bouncing checks and lying to the people and he sees many muggings and rapes through his telescope.

"What he learns isn't the whole truth about us. He reads about a new hospital and a food-for-the-needy program. He sees about a bunch of people risking their own lives to help a little kid trapped in a well on TV. He sees somebody giving a homeless person a clean safe place to stay through his telescope. It balances very well, but he can't decide whether to take Earth in or to say we must never be allowed to associate with decent people. He's torn.

"He decides to take one last look through his telescope, and what he sees is going to make his decision for him.

"He sees a homeless black man and a poor white man walking toward one another on the city street."

Billy looked expectant for a long minute, then asked, "Then what happened?"

"It hasn't happened yet," Nick said. "You figure it out. Think of what kinds of good or bad things might happen when those uneducated poor underprivileged people meet. Positive or negative?"

"I see!" Billy cried. "If they help each other, everybody

gets to go all over the universe, and if they try to rob each other, we never get to go anyplace!"

"That's right," Lonnie said. "It's a lot more subtle, when you think about it. What's really important? What tears us down?

"Think about this: What if the two men just pass each other by, and the white says, `Damned nigger!' as they get close together or the black man makes a remark about white trash honkies?"

"They'd fight."

"Think about something more subtle than that," Nick argued. "What if they don't fight. They just make a remark and keep right on walking."

"Then nothing would happen, because the guy in the UFO couldn't hear them with a telescope," Billy answered. "Would he have to look somewhere else?"

"Certainly not! He'd have the answer as to what would happen if he brought Earth into the galactic society!" Lonnie said. "He has a super futuristic telescope that lets him hear, too."

"I don't know."

"The black man and the white man are both members of the human race," Nick said. "Their skin's a little different shade. The man in the UFO learns that an almost unnoticeable thing like that means they can't get along – and he is *not* a member of the human race, or even a mammal, say. He's a whole lot different."

"Oh, yeech! It's like Dad always says. If my sister and I can't get along, how can we ever hope to get along in the world with strangers! We're the same family!"

"Now, do you understand what I meant by diminishing the entire race when you do something that hurts somebody else?" Nick asked. "Do you see how even some little thing you don't even think about can hurt everyone?"

"Yeah! You're cool! You're almost as cool as Lonnie! I got to finish collecting. See ya!"

He rode off. Lonnie looked at Nick, and said, "You're a lot deeper than I would've thought. You probably taught the kid a valuable lesson."

"You're a hell of a lot deeper than anyone gives you credit for being, too. I think we're going to end up being friends, don't you?"

Lonnie grinned.

They talked a few minutes about the various people involved in the case, then Nick got back to his car in time to get a call on the radio. Marsha said to get to Elise Norton's place right away. She'd been attacked.

Lonnie heard the message, and jumped into Nick's car as he started off.

"Mrs. Norton? Why would anyone want to hurt her?"

"Because the killer thinks she knows a hell of a lot more than she does. Either that or ... something else."

He grabbed the radio and asked what the situation was.

"She called, asked for you, and said she'd been attacked," Marsha replied. "She didn't know who did it because he was wearing a black jumpsuit and a black ski mask. She said she's injured pretty badly. She managed to do a little damage herself, in return."

"It happened in the last few minutes? The past half hour?"

"No. Before daylight this morning. She's been unconscious.

"I called the paras. They're on their way. David Klein was with the lab crew while Tiny's in court, so he's run over there across the Parks' yard. He'll beat you to her place."

Nick swung into the Norton drive just then. The car wasn't even fully stopped before Lonnie was running for the house. Nick jumped out and was at his heels.

The front door was locked, but Dr. Klein yelled the back was open. They ran around to see the screen ripped out and the catch broken in.

"I didn't stop to look for a key," Klein said, coming into the kitchen from a hallway. "It was locked, so I got in the best way I could. Doors don't just pop open in real life like they do on TV. I'm pretty sure I broke something in my shoulder.

"Where the hell is that ambulance!? She's lost one hell of a lot of blood!"

"Is she conscious?" Nick asked.

"Not at the moment. She's a *very* cool customer! She took a Xanax to lower blood loss when she called Marsha.

"Her assailant was about six feet, medium build. That's all she knows, except she stuck him in the left biceps with a letter opener.

"He tried to strangle her first, then stabbed her three times with the letter opener she stuck him with. She decided she'd play dead and dropped. He ran out."

The ambulance screamed into the drive and Klein went to the front door to speed them up and to yell for the plasma and oxygen.

"She knows a good bit about medicine, it appears," Klein said, coming back into the kitchen. "I hear she gave Tiny some lessons!"

They chatted nervously a few minutes before the paramedics brought her out on a Gurney. As they were passing, she opened her eyes, looked up at them, smiled at Lonnie, and said, "Lt. Storie, they were in time. I'll recover fully. Please see that my house is locked securely when you leave.

"Young lady! Don't *ever* again let me see you handle a needle that way! You gamble with the patient as well as with yourself! Hold it straight up and depress the plunger slowly. *Never* flick a needle with your finger! A scratch can be fatal these days! I'd demand that you concentrate on me instead of our Pan, but you're merely human – and female!

"Well? Are we to dawdle until I bleed to death or shall we get to an emergency facility? My tetanus is up to date, so we can skip that.

"Lt. Storie? My house? The locks?"

"Lonnie dear, you can't begin to know how wonderful an old woman feels when a god takes time to care.

"Well? Are we going, or not?"

The paramedic gave her a shot. She flashed them a triumphant little smile and closed her eyes, then opened them again to request, "Allan should be home tonight, Lonnie. Would you be a dear and tell Gina to fix him some supper? Tell her I'll be released in about seventy two hours, quite probably. My little injuries aren't terribly debilitating.

"Allan's my husband, Lt. Storie. Like most men, he's absolutely helpless without a woman to do for him.

"May I call you Nick? Call me Elise."

She closed her eyes again and began to snore.

"Elise, you can call me anything you want!" Nick said.

"I think I'd better ride with her to the hospital on the EMS ambulance," Dr. Klein requested. "I'd better get an X-ray of this shoulder.

"Nick, there's nothing in there to help. The attacker took the letter opener with him and there isn't any blood sample to type. Tell the lab crew working over at the Lefkowicz place to finish with the processing and give the info to me in my office. I think a TV camera – or two of them – were up in that vent space at Lefkowicz's place, so we might have a repressed voyeur type."

Nick said he'd tell them and Klein went out. Lonnie said he had some tools on his truck he could use to fix the door for Elise. Nick went into the bedroom to look for Mrs. Norton's keys to take to her while Lonnie took his car to get the tools. He went on through the house and found where the assailant had broken in through a french window in the library. It had a simple drop catch. A card or thin knife would open it easily. There wasn't anything for the lab to check on there, so he closed it and vowed to tell Allan to put a pressure spring on it to secure it when it was locked. The attacker knew about that window. He'd been in the house.

Nick located the keys and a purse, picked up a bathrobe and some clothes to take to her, then waited until Lonnie returned to put the stuff in his car. He was preparing to drive on over to the Lefkowicz house when he had an idea, so he went through the pass in the hedge.

There were older shoe prints from when Klein went through toward Norton's – and one clear ribbed print going toward the Parks'. Nick avoided it carefully and went through to get the lab crew to cast and photograph the shoe print before they left. He gave them Dr. Klein's message, then went back with Frog into the pass. They checked around until Frog found a partial ribbed toe print near the hedge about three feet from the pass. It was pointing toward the hedge.

Nick grinned at Frog and went to the hedge at the tip of the shoe print. It was almost too thick to reach into. He parted it in several places, grunted, held it open and instructed, "Frog, my friend, take a photo of the letter opener Mrs. Norton stuck into her attacker and he stuck into her! Mark this spot and have the crew get what they need and get the opener out of there. I'll see you back at the station."

He went back to help as Lonnie did a very professional job of fixing Elise's broken door, took Lonnie and the tools back to Lonnie's truck, then headed for the station – after telling Lonnie not to tell anyone Mrs. Norton was still alive, and he was definitely not to tell anyone she'd been able to speak to them.

He quickly called Marsha and had her get in touch with Dr. Klein and the paras to tell them the same thing. He didn't want the killer to run.

Now for motive. He thought he knew who the killer was. That stab wound was going to prove it.

"Doc, do you know enough psychology to help me sort a couple of things out?" Nick asked of Dr. Klein, back at the station. He'd dropped off the clothes, purse and keys to Elise at the hospital and had brought Klein back to South Station with him. Klein had a separated shoulder, but no break. It would be sore for awhile.

"You'll see all the evidence. There was at least one small TV camera in that cross vent, probably two. Mrs. Lefkowicz was the obvious subject of a rather twisted voyeur who is stimulated by Reubenesque women. I can't figure why he would kill her."

"Because she discovered his cameras and was going to sic her trucker husband on him, I'd say. Were the cameras broadcast or camcorder?"

"Camcorder. The broadcast would never get out of that vent."

"So our killer probably went in to reload his cameras and she was laying for him."

"How do you figure that? How did he get in? There wasn't any evidence of B and E."

"She met with Mrs. Norton's protest groups whenever they paraded around the neighborhood with their causes.

So did the killer. They met at her house sometimes and he knew about the key under the geranium, so getting in was easy enough. They sometimes met at Elise's, so he knew about the cheap catch-locks on the tall French windows.

"Mrs. Lefkowicz called an electrician to come to check her wall switches in the bathroom and bedroom. They made a humming noise. The way I piece it together, she noticed the noise didn't come directly from the switches, but from a vent above the switches. Maybe the cameras vibrating inside the vent.

"She was supposed to go with Elise to a community meeting about the incinerator or women's rights or something, but she cancelled and stayed home with the lights out to see who put those cameras in the vent. When the killer showed up, she confronted him and ended up dead.

"The killer knew about the new bed being dug in the Parks' back yard. He'd come through the cut in the hedge from Hotchkis, where he lives, down along Kenworth Drive, and through the Parks' yard, so he knew they weren't home.

"He carried her over there and had only dug part of the grave when his luck suddenly soured. He dropped the body into the shallow hole and stepped through the hedge to Norton's to wait until the Parks went to bed. Elise Norton drove in and he was in her headlights for a full two or three seconds.

"He dodged back through the pass, tearing the sack he had the things he'd collected with his cameras at Jeannie's. He did pick up most of it, but it was dark, and he didn't dare to use much light there, so he missed the fabric piece he'd used to cover the grille in the bathroom and a little piece of the plastic package the videotape came in.

"I suppose those phone slips blew in there long ago. It

wouldn't be too likely they were so bleached with one watering.

"Another big dilemma! Elise would be sitting over there in her kitchen for god knows how long and she'd see his light, sooner or later.

"He covered the body with what mixture was dug out and hoped Lonnie would plant the vegetables without digging there anymore, in which case he wouldn't go the sixteen or eighteen inches to the body.

"His luck stinks. Lonnie turns in the humus to that depth, so he found the body a few hours later.

"The killer was still safe – unless Elise Norton had gotten a good look at him standing by the hedge pass when she came in, so he decided to not take any chances.

"Elise is one hell of a lot more solid and determined than he ever counted on, but he's not an experienced killer, so he botched it when he left her for dead. She had stuck him with the letter opener, but her testimony's vital to proving that so we let him think she's dead.

"I want to sew this thing up tight here, then I'll go arrest him."

"You told me earlier you had it down to two people," Klein agreed. "You've obviously halved that suspect list now, so was it Shank or Walters?"

"Shank drove by with his wife while I was talking to Lonnie half an hour before we ever learned Elise had been attacked. He waved at us."

"So? I think you've lost me on this one."

"Shank was driving. He reached his arm outside the window and waved."

"And? I ... ahha! He was driving, so he reached his left arm out the window and waved at you! If he'd been recently stabbed in the left biceps, one thing he wouldn't and *couldn't* do is reach that arm out a car window to wave!

"So you will now get a murder warrant and arrest Victor Walters – *if* Walters has some difficulty maneuvering his left arm.

"Elise seemed to think her Pan god was also somehow involved in the motive. She'll be relieved to know he wasn't."

"Lonnie? I never believed for a second he was involved. He's got rules, one of which is never messing with married women. Jeannie Lefkowicz was married."

"He doesn't break his little rules?"

"It would never occur to him. Why have a rule if it doesn't mean anything?"

"So! How do you intend to handle the show, Nick?" Paddy asked. "You've always said a murder should be solved within seventy two hours or it starts getting difficult. This time, it looks like you've actually made it!"

The team were in a planning session in Paddy's office. Ed had finished his case, but Marsha and Paddy had to be back in court at two.

"Ed and I can't take the warrant over there and arrest him yet. As to the seventy two hour rule, I generally solve them in a lot less. It's getting proof that hangs me up for days or worse. Maybe we could get a state constitutional amendment through that would allow us to arrest people as soon as we get a little suspicious they maybe-might have done something or other at sometime in their life."

"Been reading the newspaper again?" Marsha asked. "I saw that. They try to hide that stuff next to the classifieds so no one sees them."

"What did I miss?" Ed asked.

"The supreme court made another ruling about warrants. It doesn't matter much anymore if a warrant's issued for some other person at some other address in some other state if us cops break down your door and hold you and your wife and kids at gunpoint, handcuff you, put your kids into therapy for the next ten years and cause your father to have a fatal heart attack. We're not responsible and can use anything we find while searching your house against you, but only if we say we did it in good faith – whatever that means."

"I'm sure you've misread it," Paddy protested.

"It would be most difficult to argue the decision was less, if you mean that thing about Jane Doe versus Murchison

County," Ed replied. "There were four dissenting votes, but this supreme court's so badly stacked now in what is called a `conservative' posture it's unlikely the direction of concerted attacks on the Constitution will lessen anytime soon."

"We don't need a new amendment!" Nick cried (They were baiting Paddy. They knew he was a staunchly loyal Republican who would never admit to the extreme excesses of the party anymore than Marsha, an equally staunch Democrat, would ever admit to the excesses of her party). "The way that thing was worded, they've redefined the words `Due process' to mean whatever some jerk-off deputy may think at any given moment."

"The beauty of it is all we have to do is produce one officer who'll claim he *thought* they were following the rules!" Marsha declared. "I think we're perfectly within the law to arrest and jail each and every suspect in each and every case and hold them in solitary until the case is solved."

"May I say that I believe we should also have the acquiescence of the courts to actually execute any murderer or other type capital offender when we're sure in our own minds he's guilty," Ed said, in his very correct way. "Perhaps we could decide such things by a simple plurality of votes of the officers assigned to the case in point."

"All right! That's going a lot too far!" Paddy said, with a grin. "You clowns get to work.

"Ha! *That's* an order I'll never see carried out!"

"Nick, what do you really think of that kind of moronic crap?" Marsha asked, ignoring Paddy. "You never get into our political arguments."

"Me? They should make it even harder for us cops to grab people or property on the whim of some jackass political hack who's mainly trying to cover his ass. I also think they should get rid of some of the more ridiculous technicalities, although there's an easy way around a lot of them."

"Uh-oh, you!" Paddy said. "What do you intend doing? What *else* did we miss?"

"If Walters doesn't come out somehow to where we can show he's got an injured arm we can't get a warrant."

"What do you mean?" Ed asked.

"I've already eliminated everyone but Shank and Walters by a process of my own. To get a warrant, we now have to prove it to a judge. I can't do that in this case. No judge is going to listen after the simplest of all arguments against the warrant comes up – and the judge is going to ask that question."

"Which is?" Paddy asked.

"Can you demonstrate, reasonably, that no other person could have committed the crime?"

"Oh, lordy-lord!" Marsha cried. "You can't show where anyone in this county couldn't have done it!"

"Bingo!"

"I hate this!" Paddy stormed. "Why does every damned stupid case you work on end up with everybody knowing the hell who did it, but without any damned proof for a court?!"

"Because of his own seventy two hour rule," Ed said. "He solves the case in that time, then can take months getting the proof. I must say, Nick, that sort of thing can aggravate. Lay out the case for us. Maybe we can discern that one small lead that will give us something to pursue."

"My problem comes down to two facts. Number one, the TV cameras in the vent shows it was either a pervert or psycho, which makes it, legally, an openended search for suspects that we can't use logic on. It's why I won't be able to get any warrant. Logic isn't a consideration in psycho cases.

"Number two is that very few murders are committed outside of an immediate small circle of people. In other words the victim knew the killer.

"I worked on the second fact because of the type of murder and the fact the killer knew details that only could be known by a person who knew quite a lot about the area, people and places.

"The fact that number one applies complicates matters."

"Well, the hospital got a call for Mrs. Norton," Paddy said. "They reported there was no information available on any such person at this time, then the medical examiner's office got a call. Klein said they did *not* give out information about the work there. The caller had to contact the police for any such information.

"He'll assume she's dead. We've sealed up that one in short enough time."

"Well! How're you gonna get around the fact that you've got no warrant?" Marsha asked. "Don't try to tell me you haven't figured *that* one out!"

"Cops can't do those things without warrants. *But* normal everyday citizens *can*, so if one happens to note that Walters has a sore left arm we'll have our grounds for the warrant. A considered suspicion by the investigating officer plus an apparent stab wound possibly received in an attack on a second victim is way too much coincidence for a judge to deny for lack of probable cause."

"So you have the citizen primed to say he observed Walters with a bandaged arm?" Paddy said, coldly.

"You know me better than that!" Nick retorted. "I'm going to send the citizen to find out. If Walters doesn't have a sore arm I'm having crow for dinner."

"You *will not* endanger any citizen!" Paddy ordered. "You're talking about a murderer here!"

"This particular citizen will never be in danger. It's going to be strictly a volunteer job. A number of people like Elise Norton and are outraged about that attack."

"You swear?" Paddy demanded.

"On my mother's grave!"

"Who you gonna use?" Marsha asked.

"A little kid and a god," Nick grinned and got out of there fast, waving for Ed to come along before Paddy exploded about that "little kid" being used statement.

"Lonnie, Jon, this is Ed. Ed Goins," Nick greeted, as he and Ed strolled up to where Lonnie was unloading cypress mulch into his wheelbarrow in front of Finney's place. Jon Le Bonne was standing there talking with Lonnie and watching him with a dreamy-eyed expression. Ed grinned, unusual for him. He usually kept a very bland expression, no matter the situation.

"Hi! I saw you when you and Nick were where I found the body," Lonnie greeted, offering his hand. "I saw Elise this morning. She had me on a list of people who could go in. She's fine today. Jon won't say anything. I trust him."

"We're about ready to hang our murderer, but we'll need a normal citizen's testimony for the warrant," Nick said, skipping the usual lead-in. "Can you help us? Could we get Billy Milton to help?"

"Anything! I want to get my hands on the bastard who did that to Mrs. Norton!" Lonnie said. "What do we need Billy for?"

"We need someone who has what should seem like a legitimate reason to get him outside where we can see him," Ed said. "You can be the adult citizen who notes a certain thing about him."

"The arm!" Lonnie agreed. "You don't need Billy. I can go talk about yard work with anyone I like."

"Not this one," Nick said.

"The creep? I thought so, by god!"

"I can get him out," Jon suggested. "I can claim there've been electrical problems with the aluminum wiring in these houses and I'm doing free inspections today. The part about aluminum wiring's true, so he won't be too very suspicious."

"OK. It's worth a try," Nick replied. "That way, we won't need Lonnie as an eye witness. You're adult.

"It could be dangerous, but I don't really think so – so long as you don't go inside. Stay out front and note something about him. Get him to sign something. Anything that means he has to use both his hands."

"What am I looking for?" Jon asked.

"We mustn't tell you that," Ed replied, before Lonnie could say anything. "We'll want no suggestion we asked you to note any specific trait."

"I know, but I'll shut up," Lonnie said, grinning.

They went to Jon's electrician's van and found a fill-in form about inspecting electrical systems with an estimation section beneath it. Jon looked through some rubber stamps in the jumbled glove case, stamped a big red "No Charge" on the estimate line of the top three forms, grinned, saluted and climbed into his van to go over to Walters' place. It was good luck he was the second house from the corner, because Jon parked near the corner and walked to the front door of the first house, rang the bell, talked to the lady who answered for a minute and left.

Ed "happened" to be walking by as Jon rang the front doorbell at Walters' and heard someone yell, "Who is it and what do you want?" from inside.

"I represent Le Bonne Electrical Contractors! We're checking the houses in this area because some of them have aluminum wiring and there have been some close calls with fire."

"There wasn't any aluminum wiring used in this house! I am not interested!"

"There's no charge, sir! The safety of the entire neighborhood is at stake!"

"Damn it all! This house is all copper wiring! I know! I have never trusted aluminum and I specifically contracted for copper wiring only! I'm ill! Go away!"

Jon shrugged and walked back to his van and drove off. Ed went down the block to meet Nick and Lonnie sitting in Nick's car out of sight around the corner.

"Well, it didn't work," Ed reported. "Walters refused to come to the door. He said he is ill."

"I'll get him to the door!" Lonnie promised.

"No. We'll have to use Billy," Nick said. "We just have to hope Walters takes the paper from him."

"He does. I warned Billy if that guy ever tries to get him inside the house to get away and tell me right away."

"*What*?! Do you mean the man's a child molester?!" Ed asked, shocked.

"I wouldn't be surprised, I've never seen or heard anything like that, but I do know he's a creep."

"Well, where will we find Billy?" Nick asked.

"He lives over on the next block west and a block down. If Walters is upstairs he can see the street along the front of Billy's house."

"Damn!" Ed spat. "I walked past the place, so it would be much too suspicious if I also showed up at the paperboy's house, then the paperboy went to his place."

"I go over there sometimes," Lonnie said. "I can get him."

"You're too good a friend to Elise," Nick replied. "He's *got* to be paranoid as hell about now!"

"Jon! Find Jon!" Lonnie said. "He can go along the street

and stop at Billy's house. Third or fourth stop, but that's necessary."

"Yo!" Nick said. "It would be logical. Is he at the mall?"

They drove over to find Jon at the store and explained what they needed. Jon was willing to do *anything* that Lonnie asked him to do.

An hour later, Jon went to the door of the Milton house as he advanced along the block with a clipboard, asking everyone if they'd experienced unusual power surges lately (They had. A sewer contractor had dug up a carrier cable down the block) and writing down the approximate times.

At the Milton's, he left a letter to Billy from Nick asking him to ride his bike down to the corner of Kenworth and Iris Way, where Ed, Lonnie and he had a little side-job for him to do. Mrs. Milton was suspicious, so Jon told her Nick was the police and that Lonnie was helping them with the murder case.

Mrs. Milton, like every other woman in the area (and Jon) melted when it was something Lonnie wanted. She also knew Lonnie wouldn't permit Billy to be put in any dangerous situation, so she said Billy would be there.

Jon went to one more house, then got in his van and drove off. Billy rode his bike to the corner, where Nick explained what they needed.

"Billy, this isn't a game," Lonnie warned. "We all think the creep is the one who stabbed Mrs. Norton and we want his ass! We have to make him come outside where we can see him. Can you say you're collecting for the paper or something?"

"He sends a check, He paid this month."

"Sheee! What can we do now?" Lonnie asked.

"I know! I'll tell him that his check bounced again!" Billy said, eagerly. "He sent one once before and forgot to sign it and it bounced!"

"That ought to do it, but he might simply yell that he'll send you another one," Ed said.

"He's scared of cops? I'll fix him! I can get him to come out fast!"

"Billy, don't you try to be a hero!" Lonnie demanded. "Remember this; he *killed* Mrs. Lefkowicz! Stay at least ten feet away from him. You have to promise."

Billy sobered up and looked a little worried. "I thought he only stabbed Mrs. Norton. I'll be careful, Lon. Just tell me what to do."

"Get him outside where we can see and try to get him to sign something or lift something," Nick suggested.

"Okay."

"We'll find a place to hide where we can watch you," Ed promised. "Stay away from him. If he tries to grab you, run. If you hear Nick or myself yell to drop, do it right then. Don't think. Fall and lay as flat on the ground as you can!"

"Sheee! I might be in a shootout?!" Billy asked, eyes wide and bright.

"It'll be a short one," Nick replied. "I don't think there's going to be any trouble, but we do have to be ready. If he even looks like he's going to attack you I'll put six slugs right through his damned head and explain later!"

Billy gave them a sickly grin. Lonnie hugged him tightly around the shoulders and said there wouldn't be any trouble because the creep didn't have the guts. He couldn't even handle Mrs. Norton.

"I can take us in through the Kile's place on Kenwood, through the pass to the Ling's in the next house and along. It's got that big hedge to within fifty feet from his door," Lonnie said to Nick. "He can't see us there, so Billy should give us about ten minutes, then go on in. There isn't any pass to any neighbors from his place, which shows how much they all like him."

They told Billy to wait, then drove around the block and to the place behind Walters' to run through the yard. Mrs. Kile saw them and came out, but when she saw Lonnie she smiled and waved.

Billy was just turning into Walters' front walk as they reached their position by the hedge. They watched him walk up and ring the bell.

"Who is it? What do you want?" they heard from inside.

"It's Billy! Your check bounced!"

"That is not true! I have plenty to cover my checks!" Walters yelled back.

"You didn't sign it! I got to pay for my new Nintendo! I want my money!"

"Stop yelling! I'll send you another check!"

"I want my money *right now* or I'll tell the cops you gave me another bad check!" Billy yelled, angrily. "You did the same thing before! You just want to screw me out of my money! Mom says you probably kite checks all the time! I want what you owe right now!"

"All right! All right! How much is it? I'll pay cash."

"Eleven seventy five!"

There was a couple minutes' pause, then the door opened and Walters stepped out to hand Billy a ten and two ones.

"Keep the change for your trouble. I'll see the checks are signed. It was merely an oversight.

"I'm very ill. I can't stand this!"

"Geez! What happened to you? You look really awful! I'm sorry. I didn't know you were sick. I could wait a little longer. It's not *that* important."

"It's all right. I know how important it is that one pays one's bills on time. I'll simply have to rest for awhile."

"Sheee! You should see a doctor! You look really awful!

What did you do to your arm?"

"I cut it on a rusty nail and got an infection. I'm going to the doctor with it. I think I need a shot."

Nick could see Walters was extremely pale and sweating and unsteady on his feet. The arm was wrapped in a white bandage and was in a makeshift sling.

Lonnie broke around the hedge, looked over to the two by the door and called, "Hi, Billy! How's it going?"

"Hey, Lon! I think Mr. Walters is real sick!" Billy called back. "He should go to a doctor."

"Your mom told me if I saw you anywhere to tell you your distributor called and said the bank passed that check and you've got the money. The guy forgets to sign checks all the time.

"Mr. Walters, you look to be in bad shape. Can I take you to the hospital?"

"Oh, god! Why don't you put on some clothes?" Walters said. "Don't you know what people think, seeing you half-naked like that? It's downright indecent!"

"I'm very sick. I have an infection. I can't ... oh, god!"

"You have an infected stab wound in your arm, don't you, Mr. Walters?"

"You know. You know everything. You always know everything. Yes, I have a stab wound. It all came apart and I have a stab wound that's infected.

"Oh, god! I'm so screwed up! I can't be this way! I can't *be* this way! It's wrong! It's sinful!"

He swayed and his eyes started to become unfocused. He shook his head, then looked at Lonnie. "It's blood poisoning. Staphylococcus. The streaks are terrible. I've watched them spread toward my heart.

"I hope I die! I swear before God I never meant for anything like this evil to happen! I didn't want to hurt anyone! I swear to god I never meant to hurt anyone!

"Oh, god! I love you! I can't help if I...."

He swayed. Lonnie caught him as Nick and Ed came around the hedge.

"Ed, call an ambulance," Nick ordered. "Billy, this worked better than I thought it would. I'm sorry you saw and heard this."

"Gee! Mr. Walters didn't mean to kill Mrs. Lefkowicz or hurt Mrs. Norton, huh? Nick, I know what you and Lon were telling me yesterday. I don't feel like a big hero because we caught a killer. I feel just awful!"

Tears were starting to run down his face. Lonnie laid Walters on the sidewalk and pulled Billy to him.

"The whole damned race was diminished, wasn't it? The whole damned race was wounded, not only Elise and Mrs. Lefkowicz. Every one of us is less.

"He probably didn't really mean to kill Mrs. Lefkowicz, but he damned well went over to Mrs. Norton's to kill her."

"Yes. I was totally out of control by then," Walters agreed, weakly. "I didn't mean to hurt Jeannie, but she was hiding there and jumped out at me. I pushed her and she fell, then she started swearing and calling me a.... I tried to explain. She kept calling me a pervert. I grabbed her arm and she slapped me. I hit her. She started to scream and I choked her. I couldn't stop myself! I squeezed and squeezed and I couldn't stop!"

He closed his eyes. "I wish I was dead!" he whispered. "I was only trying to stop. I was only trying to stop. I couldn't stop thinking about you and I couldn't stop choking her. I could never stop! Never in my life could I *stop*!"

"About me?" Lonnie asked. "You thought about me while you were choking her? But *why*?"

"Not then. Before. All the time. I think about you and

dream about you and want you."

"But *why*?" Lonnie asked again.

"You really don't have a clue, do you? You don't even *know*!" Walters cried, staring very clear-eyed at Lonnie. "Because it's not just something Elise said in passing while talking with those women. It's not only an expression. You *are* Pan! You're not indecent or immoral, like I thought. You're merely unmoral.

"I'm sorry about Elise. She was a very good person."

"She'll be all right," Nick told him. "She'll be home in a couple more days."

"I'm so relieved! I hated myself all the time because I thought...." He passed out just as the Emergency Squad paramedics' van screeched to a halt at the sidewalk.

"Lonnie, take Billy home, will you?" Nick asked. "You can use my car."

"I'm okay," Billy said. "I've got my bike."

"Why did Mr. Walters think he had to hurt anyone just because he loves Lonnie? He didn't know it's alright?"

"It is?!" Ed asked, clearly confused.

"Lonnie loves everybody, so it's all right if you love him back," Billy said, simply.

"It's not that kind of love he was talking about," Nick said.

"Strangely, it was," Walters corrected him. Nick turned to see him being loaded onto a stretcher. He was conscious and listening. "I ... I didn't know it ... until this moment, but it was really the love of a beautiful thing.

"He's Pan, son. Even the sexual part really is alright to think about. I never stopped to think I was adding that when it wasn't really there at first – because I was terrified. Pan is a purely sexual being. It's a part of the whole idea of even having a Pan that he...." he trailed off again, then opened his eyes to add, "All I really wanted was for him to hold me the way he's holding you right now and say I wasn't that my ... that my life wasn't wasted.

"Pan, I was always ... afraid to say anything to you. I was terrified you'd seduce me. The first time I saw you at work across the street there, I couldn't even breathe! I felt you could seduce me with a word or a look, so I desperately tried to maintain a safe distance so you couldn't."

"I never realized that you already had!" He said that in awed wonderment, then passed out again.

"What does that mean?" Lonnie asked.

"Is Mr. Walters gay?" Billy asked.

"I'd say he probably is, but he never knew it until he saw Lonnie across the street," Ed said. "He was trying not to be."

"But why did he kill Mrs. Lefkowicz?" Billy asked. "Lonnie says some people are gay and some aren't. Like Jon is and he isn't. He can still be Jon's good friend, because all anyone has to do is say no."

"What does he mean I seduced him?" Lonnie demanded. "I never even talked to him before!"

"Because someone's seduced the moment they decide they'll do a thing, whether they ever actually do it or not," Nick said. "This is going to be complicated, but I have to sort it out."

"Is Mr. Walters going to get the chair now?" Billy asked.

"No, Billy. He'll probably have to get medical treatment," Nick answered. "He might have to serve some time, but he's got a screwed-up head. He really never did mean to hurt anyone."

"I'm glad," Billy replied, seriously. "We were all wrong to call him a creep, weren't we Lon?"

"Yes. Very. We were who walked by when the guy from the UFO was watching. We made the vicious remark. It was me all along, and I couldn't see it."

"I still feel awful," Billy said.

"You have to never forget this," Nick said. "If you learned something here that you can use to help make yourself a better person, everything's not lost."

Billy nodded. "I think I want to be a cop. I want to be like you, Nick. As everyone says, it wouldn't hurt anything to look like Lonnie, either!"

"I think Lonnie wouldn't look so good if he didn't have what makes him Lonnie inside," Ed said.

"Hell! Now *you're* talking in riddles!" Lonnie accused.

"I know what he means!" Billy said. "I better go on home and tell mom everything turned out okay. If I tell her the truth she'll worry."

He trotted to his bike and sped away with a backward wave.

"That kid's at least fifty!" Ed said.

"I spend my entire damned life not knowing what the hell's going on!" Lonnie complained.

"You *do* know what's going on about everything except yourself, Pan," Nick said. "I think I'll go to the hospital and talk with Elise. Want to come along?"

"Might as well.The day's shot to hell and back now, anyhow."

"Lonnie, dear! How sweet of you to come again!" Elise announced, with her little knowing smile. "Hello Lt. Storie."

"We agreed I'd call you Elise and you'd call me Nick."

"We did?" she said, with the smile. "I'm glad.

"Hello there, Nick. Have you learned anything new?"

"We learned it was Victor Walters and we already caught him," Lonnie answered. "Killing Mrs. Lefkowicz was sort of an accident. He lost control, somehow. Now he has blood poisoning. Pretty bad."

"Blood poisoning? You mean staph infection?"

"The wound on his arm infected," Nick agreed. "He's pretty badly screwed up, in a number of ways."

"Why did he kill her? Do you know that?"

"As soon as he's able, he'll tell me the whole story," Nick said. "Somehow, it was because he thought he was in love with Pan. He was fighting the fear he's homosexual."

"In love with Lonnie? Hmm. He isn't very stable, but I suppose he could be actually in love with Lonnie. Everyone else is. That's the whole point of even having a Pan!"

"It's my point, too," Nick replied. "He's in love with a myth. He's projected Pan into Lonnie."

"No. No. Lonnie is Pan, Nick," she said, laying back on the pillows, with her knowing smile. "You have to see it like it is. Otherwise you'll never have a faint hope to understand what's going on around Lonnie."

"Hell! I never even know what's going on around myself!" Lonnie exclaimed. "What's all this stuff?"

"I know, dear. I'll try to explain what I mean.

"Pan isn't a being, he's an idea. He's an ideal everybody can use to build wild fantasies around. He's something totally unbounded by normal convention or rules, something we can use to fantasize about the things we're inhibited or prohibited against ever experiencing.

"You're the most beautiful man most people ever saw. You have the form of the famous David statue and finer features than an artist could portray. In addition, you're a very honest and caring person. You're a little shy and you're a true innocent in an age when there simply *are* no more innocents!

"Pan exists as an ideal. You're the focus of that ideal. You, therefore, take on all the characteristics of the ideal to the point none of us can see those things about you that are *not* part of the concept.

"You become, as a direct result, truly Pan. You're the randy, unmoral, delightful, uninhibited god we've made you. The proof you're mortal is that you so steadfastly refuse to do anything with any married women, which was certainly not any least part of the classical Pan, but we married women still dream of you.

"You probably don't often sleep with men, but we can forgive that, because Pan has no inhibitions. He is required by what he is to teach sexual techniques to anybody, male or female."

"I don't ever sleep with men!" Lonnie cried.

"But you don't see anything wrong with it, now do you?"

"Well, no. Not really. I mean, if two men want to why shouldn't they? I just don't want to."

"You never think about what it would be like to go to bed with your friend, Jon?"

He blushed and grinned. She turned on her knowing smile.

"Do you see what happened to Walters?" Nick asked.

"He wondered what it would be like to go to bed with me?" Lonnie asked.

"Yes, dear." Elise replied. "He ended up taking it quite a lot further than that. He had started worrying that the fact he even wondered about it might mean he actually wanted to do it. He's terribly repressed about sin and all that rot, so he began to feel he was evil and less a man, then he projected the evil to you and you became an obsession. He didn't understand it's very natural to react to beauty like that. You'll find he thought you were trying to seduce him. Bet on it. I've seen this sort of thing before, if not nearly to such an extreme."

"I'll be damned! That's exactly what he said!" Lonnie cried.

"Once you make him understand what he felt was only normal, he'll feel far less threatened to himself and will take the silly 'evil' back, at the same time. The next step will be for him to understand that there is no evil in the situation. Pan does things that are forbidden, but not things that are wrong. He is above right and wrong."

"Unmoral, not immoral.".

"That's the crux of the matter, isn't it?"

"He passed that crux," Nick said. "He realizes his initial response to Lonnie wasn't sexual. It was simply his wanting to be close to the ideal."

"How did he express that bit?" Elise asked. "I worked in a psychiatric ward for four years. I have some small idea of how these things go."

"Billy Milton, the paperboy, got him to come outside with a ruse," Nick said. "He found it's no picnic playing those games. I'll admit I miscalculated there, but I think he'll be alright. He understands more than we do, I think.

"Lonnie was holding Billy, telling him why we had to do that trick. Walters said all he ever wanted really was for Lonnie to hold him and tell him his life wasn't a waste."

"Don't you see what he wanted? He merely wanted to be enfolded in the closest thing to perfection he'd ever seen and to receive some kind of validation. That's all the whole bunch of us foolish women want – to be able to actually touch perfection and to have our Pan tell us we're important to him. That Lonnie came here to see me proves so much to me!"

"Well, I'll want to stop by emergency to see how Walters is getting along," Nick said. "I'll leave you two to chat, then I'll come back."

"Tell him I'll get in to see him later when they let me be ambulatory," Elise said. "I really do understand a little of what he was going through, but he does owe me an apology."

"I'll tell him," Nick said and went to the desk to ask where Walters was. The nurse checked his police credentials and told them Walters was in three fifteen, but he wasn't yet conscious.

"According to the computer they had to do a direct major veinal strip in one place. "It was resistant. He's under some stronger anesthesia. He can answer questions tomorrow."

Nick went back to Elise's room to chat awhile longer, then took Lonnie back to his truck. He agreed they'd get together for a fishing trip after the Walters mess was over.

"Bring a girlfriend," Nick said, with a grin. "My desires for Pan don't extend past thinking you're a fairly nice guy."

"Maybe I'll bring Jon," Lonnie said, returning the grin. "Mrs. Norton says it will be alright if I do sleep with him because that's part of what's expected of me."

"Okay! Consider Janet, my fiancee, as married – and *don't* pay any attention to what Elise might have said about Pan not being restricted from married women!"

"Sheesh! You take all the fun out of life! I suppose I can finish mulching these beds and finish tomorrow."

Nick went to the station, filed his report, and went on home. Tomorrow he might even find out what this thing was really about! He'd heard a lot about psychological problems, but this was the first one he'd encountered where he could make any real decision as to whether it was purely bunk or had a basis.

Somehow, he thought it wasn't purely bunk. Always.

"Well! You do get a bit dramatic now and again, don't you?" Paddy accused at their debriefing in his office the next morning. "You better thank whatever gods you believe in that kid wasn't harmed! I'd have your ass!"

"Billy's a smart kid. He wasn't in any danger so long as he did what we said," Nick replied. "As soon as Lonnie saw him getting too close he went right out there to protect him.

"He was never placed in any danger. Walters had already decided it was over. He'd have to go to a doctor with the arm, and we'd have him, or lay there and die."

"Do you think he can make the psycho defense stick?" Marsha asked.

"The truth? Yes. I do think it's a legitimate defense, at this point. He was screwed up."

"I have to agree," Ed said. "I'm not a bleeding heart, but the man was really impaired mentally by his innate fears."

"I'm usually the one who scoffs at the psychobabble defense ploy," Paddy said. "Marsha usually bleeds tears all over the place for some of the scum we get through here.

"So you've decided not to fight that defense?"

"I've decided to have a talk with him about it. What he tells me and whether or not I believe him will decide it. I think I see why he was so messed up. I can understand it."

"Do you find yourself attracted to Lonnie, Nick?" Ed asked, seriously. "Does that tend to tell you how the fellow may have been affected?"

"Well, yes, in a way. I remember the first impact he had. It wasn't sexual with me, I don't think, but he does hit you like a two ton weight, doesn't he?"

"I have *got* to meet this guy!" Marsha said.

"He had a very sudden impact on me," Ed agreed. "I felt he was ... innocent. He's got those women chasing him around and that Jon fellow would slit his wrists if Lonnie said he'd like to see that. I don't doubt he's the most dangerous character I've ever seen, yet I felt some kind of awe or something being close to him. As silly as it may sound coming from such as me, I think perhaps Mrs.

Norton is one hundred percent correct. He *is* Pan!"

"Say what?" Marsha asked.

"He isn't dangerous, but he could be," Nick replied. "And I agree. If you accept the premise that Pan is a concept, he's very definitely Pan."

"I'm not talking about any concept," Ed said, soberly. "If you show up over there tomorrow and he's disappeared from the face of the Earth I won't bat an eye! I won't be surprised for a single second! I mean he *is* Pan!

"Saints preserve us! I'm as nuts as Walters!"

"Hello. How are you feeling today, Mr. Walters?" Nick greeted the next morning in Walter's hospital room. "I'm Det. Lt. Nick Storie. You may not remember me from yesterday's confusion."

"I remember, in a vague sort of way. I can't say I feel at all well. I think I've confessed to several things, haven't I?"

"Yes, you have. They didn't really matter. Your stab wound proves our case.

"You can have a lawyer present while we talk, if you'd like. I need some answers."

"I have no intention of presenting any defense. I killed Jeannie and tried to kill Elise.

"Elise came to see me about half an hour ago. She first demanded an apology. When I gave it, she forgave me and decided that closes the matter. She also told me I'd spilled my guts about other things and told me I'm six kinds of damned fool – a conclusion I'd already reached.

"She's an amazing woman."

"That's one place you get no argument from me, whatever. I think you should present a defense. You were mentally impaired."

"No. I was severely emotionally impaired. Elise told me to claim extenuating circumstances.

"You see, I fancied myself being in love with Lonnie Micks, which meant I'm homosexual, which meant I'm a lost sinner. My strict puritanical upbringing, therefore, damned me, no matter what I did. I was fighting something that's a part of me."

"Are you certain you're gay? Lonnie doesn't count, if you can believe Elise."

"My next great confusion! I don't know. Elise said it wasn't sex I wanted with him."

"Well, she's wrong. She can tell you what a woman feels, but she can't know what a man feels. I'll agree that sex isn't the *only* thing you wanted from him. It isn't even the major thing.

"Pan, as she sees him, is a purely sexual being. I tend to agree Lonnie's as close to Pan as anyone could be."

"Do you feel a sexual attraction to him?"

"The truth? I don't really know. I like him. He's honest and he cares. He's very intelligent, you know. I like being with him."

"He's also an exceptional artist. Look at what he does with plants! That's part of the myth. Pan is one with nature."

"Yes. Which surely means there can be no wrong or sin attached to whatever you might feel toward him. He's a sort of elemental.

"Now that we've bared our true souls to one another, take me through the whole thing, okay?"

Walter's closed his eyes for a few seconds, then began: "The first time I saw Lonnie Micks, he was working across the street, unloading sacks of gravel for the walk. It was about noon or shortly before and it was rather hot. The sun was straight above. His truck was parked under the large oak by the sidewalk. He was dressed as he always seems to be. He was sweating just enough that, when he stepped into the sunlight, he glistened and glowed a light golden brown. The young paperboy, Billy, was walking along to one side looking at him in awe, like he was seeing a god.

"He turned to profile from my perspective, looking back toward Billy while saying something that ended in a laugh.

"It was much like being hit in the stomach with a board!

I couldn't breathe! He was far the most magnificent sight I'd ever seen or dared to imagine!

"He turned toward me, noticed me, and smiled. I was suddenly frozen, terrified! I couldn't understand what it was I was feeling. I wanted to run to him, to kneel at his feet. I was panicked and wanted to flee, at the same time. I saw a god and I saw Satan incarnate. I turned and fled in sheer terror back inside my house, where I became physically ill. I believed he was trying to seduce me and to sexually take me and use me, which was damnation for my eternal soul. I wanted him to, at the same time. It terrified me.

"I realize now it wasn't a true sexual attraction, then. I twisted it around to where it probably was, later, because I.... Let me start perhaps two weeks before that. Maybe I was brainwashed by events into my reaction – in fact, I know I was.

"Elise goes for many causes. She's passionately interested in any number of things, some of which have great merit and some of which have none whatever.

"I am a member of a small group in the near neighborhood who get together to decide which of the projects we wish to invest time and effort into.

"The first I heard of Lonnie, Alicia Hamlin – who lives over on Trenton – told the members of a fantastic new gardener who recently moved to the area. He was the perfect man in appearance, as well as a true genius and artist. She described him as having a body the Greek sculptors would die for. She said he had the most perfect teeth she'd ever seen and a face that made her feel odd things she hadn't felt since she was a teenager, yet he didn't even seem to be aware he looked like a god.

"I put it to a middle-aged woman who saw some appealing young man and had a crush on him.

"Next meeting, he'd started working for the Parks. Gina was gushing all over the place about such a `beautiful innocent.' Two of the women who weren't married said that he had reacted to their advances and had slept with them. They *still* spoke of him as shy and innocent! At the same time, they carried on scandalously about how fantastic a lover he was!

"Elise said she'd watched him working at the Parks' and had talked with him and she was convinced he was Pan.

"That's where the idea started that eventually trapped me, I think. Nobody had even considered how ridiculous such a statement had to be.

"I heard so much talk about Lonnie – or `Our Pan,' as he was always referred to at the meetings – almost to the exclusion of talk of anything else. Elise soon expanded her definition of Pan to explain Lonnie was Pan because he had all the traits of an elemental god plus the body and features of a god, thus they had actually made him into a god. Perception is reality argument.

"It was all sort of silly to me, but I figured he'd screw up, sooner or later. Everybody does.

"Then I saw him there with a ten year old child seeming to worship him.

"You know what kind of strong impact he has on people. Perhaps you can understand the combination of hearing the old myth and seeing the physical embodiment of that myth's impact on me. I'm too suggestible already, then that!

"I tried my best to avoid him, yet I could never stop myself from driving by wherever I saw his truck, just to look at him. I didn't dare to return a friendly smile or wave, fearing it would end the fantasies and would result in my actually submitting to him. I began to fear I was homosexual. My upbringing had denied me much sexual experience and I always felt badly soiled by the few times I'd known carnal knowledge of a woman. Somehow, even the most depraved disgusting things I could even conceive of seemed clean and pure if it was for Lonnie. For Pan.

"I knew Jeannie from our meetings. She had shown all of us where the emergency key to her house was. I knew her husband was away for four or five days a week and that she was often out quite late at our meetings or with her other friends.

"I wired two camcorders in the vent between the bath and the bedroom in her house and wired the cam switches to the rooms' light switches. I always have been attracted to the more voluptuous women and hoped that watching her in situations where she would be nude would turn me around, would stop me from thinking and dreaming of Pan, of Lonnie.

"I would never have allowed anyone else to see those tapes. Never. That I swear as absolute truth.

"I always wore cotton gloves when I went there. I've read enough detective novels to know a single fingerprint can locate anyone, anywhere. I vowed there would not be any such evidence to tell who emplaced the video-cameras, should they be discovered.

"It worked, to a small extent. I found seeing her in the shower or the bedroom stimulated and excited me – but each time I saw Lonnie I'd start to think of him, of having him hold me, of even what it would be like. I know he does sometimes bed males. He is close friends with that Le Bonne ... person. Le Bonne makes no secret of his homosexuality.

"It seems perfectly natural to him! I sometimes see them together, laughing and joking in total innocence. I see they are truly close friends and know Lonnie must bed him. He couldn't stand life if Pan rejected him.

"I couldn't stop thinking of Pan. I couldn't be jealous of the women or of Le Bonne. It was, after all, Pan's function to bed everyone. As Elise says so often, he *is* basically a purely sexual being.

"I was managing to exert control, to an extent. A strange sort of stability came with all that and I could find a way to function again.

"Then one of my video spy cameras had a drive gear wear and begin making slight unusual noises. Jeannie must have heard it and wondered what it could be up in that little vent, and had looked, discovering my two camcorders. She laid a clever trap and caught me.

"I didn't mean to harm her. I tried to explain to her it was because of Lonnie and she became almost insane, calling me a pervert and yelling that Lonnie didn't tell me to do anything like that. I tried to tell her Lonnie didn't know about it. It wasn't *for* him, it was *because* of him.

"She got more and more furious. She wouldn't stop calling me vile names and I was going to simply leave and take the consequences. She grabbed at me and said that her husband would cut my throat for doing that. I then grabbed her arm to simply shake her and make her stop the hysterical yelling, but she slapped me. I hit her then and she came at me, starting to scream so loudly I was afraid someone outside would hear. I grabbed at her to put my hand over her mouth, but she bit at me. I found my hand around her throat, squeezing. I ordered it to stop, but I couldn't. I just kept squeezing and begging her to stop. I must have choked her for two solid hours, but I know it wasn't even two minutes. She was dead.

"I was sick and scared. I didn't know what to do. I started to call the police twice, but hung up both times.

"I remembered that Lonnie was making a vegetable bed at the Parks' rear lawn. It occurred to me I could bury her there and no one would ever know, so I gathered all my paraphernalia from the vent into the bag of replacement tapes I brought in, obtained a large plastic garbage bag from her kitchen, bent her into it, and tied it securely, slung her across my shoulder, went out on the front porch, locked the door, and put the key back behind the geranium, waited until it was quiet and no cars were in sight, then slipped across the street and around back at the Parks'. I knew they were at the theater and wouldn't be home until late.

"I had no real idea of the time. I thought perhaps it was around nine thirty or ten, so I'd have plenty of time. I would be home and safely in bed by midnight.

"I dug a hole in the bed, being very careful to keep the soil I took from the top to one side so it wouldn't show when I put it back on top.

"Then things all started going wrong again. The Parks came home.

"I dropped the body into the shallow grave I'd dug and took up my sack. I knew the Parks went to bed early, because he's had open heart surgery. I still thought it was much earlier.

"I silently stepped through the pass in the hedge to Elise's back yard to wait until the Parks retired for the night, then I'd finish my grisly task.

"Then Elise came home! Her headlights shown directly onto me! I was frozen for what seemed like a full minute before I dashed back through the hedge.

"Elise didn't immediately come outside to check, so I covered over Jeannie's body, hoping Lonnie had finished preparing the bed and would plant things. He wouldn't find Jeannie there. The sprinklers come on automatically before dawn and would hide the fact there had been any digging.

"I couldn't stay to dig more because Elise might check at any moment. She sits in her kitchen and fills out her diary every night.

"I was leaving when I discovered my sack was torn. I went back to see I'd caught the sack in the hedge when I came out of the pass. I picked up everything I could find, then went home to cower in my bed the rest of the night, expecting the police to knock on my door at any moment.

"They didn't. I drove by the Parks' home twice in the morning, but everything seemed normal. Pan was there, working in his natural setting, creating perfection.

"Then Lonnie found the body.

"Still, there was no evidence I had anything to do with it. It was merely a body buried in a flower bed.

"I was terrified that Lonnie would be blamed. I knew I wouldn't, couldn't, ever permit any such travesty to happen. I had already altered my thinking on him enough to know he wasn't evil in any way. The evil was in such a thing as I had become. If Lonnie was suspected I was going to write a full confession and send it to the police station, then I was going to kill myself and accept eternal damnation as exactly what I deserve.

"Pan *is* innocent, you know. He has never knowingly done an evil or malicious thing.

"To my own tremendous relief he was never suspected. Gina called and said you, Lt. Storie, knew that Lonnie could never do anything like that. I would never be suspected, either, due to the fact there was no connection whatever between me and Jeannie that could serve as motive.

"I drove by and saw you crossing from Elise's place to the Parks and suddenly remembered she had seen me in her garden in the automobile headlights. I agonized greatly over the possibility that she might have recognized me, even though I was quite fully disguised. It occurred to me she had seen me in that costume two years ago when we produced a silly play where I played an environmental activist and wore it in a scene.

"Instead of waiting or turning myself in, I decided to silence her. I had become a truly evil thing by then and no longer cared. Perhaps I could lay claim that I had become unhinged, at that time, but not at the time I killed Jeannie. Though I never meant to harm Jeannie, I went to Elise's with full intent of killing her.

"Again, I proved my incompetence. She managed to stab me with a letter opener.

"I thought I had killed her. I went home, afraid to have the wound in my arm professionally disinfected and treated. The end result is laying here before you.

"If I've left anything out, ask."

"You thought I'd recognize you in that old costume?" Elise asked from behind Nick, causing both Walters and Nick to jump. "No. I didn't."

"How long have you been there?" Nick asked.

"Since the part about Victor seeing our Lonnie from across the street. I was rather blind about the effect my fantasies might have on others, wasn't I? I owe you an apology, too.

"Millie, my nurse, told me you were here, Nick, so I came on up.

"Victor, you're a total fool and you always have been. You should learn to keep your mouth shut. Nick didn't have so strong a case before you blabbered away like an idiot. Now he can get a very sure serious conviction."

"I'd be willing for him to plead for extenuating circumstances," Nick replied. "He wasn't carrying a weapon and didn't intend to kill Mrs. Lefkowicz. You've already forgiven him, so that screws up the case against him for that!"

"In other words he can enter a plea of manslaughter for Jeannie and you'll let him plea bargain for whatever he can get – and you won't bring charges about me if I ask you not to." She grinned.

"So long as he pays your hospital and recovery costs," Nick finished.

"I have an accident policy.

" Great lord! It wasn't an accident, so they'll try to avoid paying!"

"I'll give you a blank signed check," Walters declared. "I have something over sixty thousand dollars in the bank. You can use it all. I won't plea bargain."

"Victor! Stop being a complete idiot! I am *not* impressed with repentant martyr syndrome! You may have a deep psychological need to be punished, but I tend to think you've been punished enough for things you didn't do. You've punished yourself far more than anyone outside could.

"I think probably the best thing in the world for you would be for Lonnie to come in here and rape you to exhaustion! I'm going to tell him to do it!

"Stop being such a total ass! You just might find your silly fantasies turning to horror if they ever come true! That factor is the negative side of fantasies. When it comes down to the grunting and sweating, it's almost never quite the way you thought it would be."

"Do you really believe that?" Nick grinned.

"Hell, no! However, I do believe it's time that Victor woke up to reality.

"I wonder! If I told Lonnie to screw him, would he?"

"He'd say, `Well, Mrs. Norton, if you think it'll do him any good, I'll do it,'" Nick replied, dryly. "He wouldn't refrain from it if he thought refraining would hurt anyone.

"Oh, yeah. One other thing, Vic. Lonnie's never bedded Jon Le Bonne. He doesn't realize Jon's serious about wanting him to."

"It wouldn't matter to anyone but Jon if he had," Elise said. "Well, Victor? Are you going to use some common sense or am I going to have to have you declared mentally incompetent?"

"I believe you actually would do that, Elise! I even believe you could pull it off.

"Very well. I'll plead to involuntary manslaughter if it'll get you off my back for a minute or two!"

"That's what it was, you silly twit! Why don't you keep your tetanus up to date? You could end up with lockjaw!"

"It was staphylococcus, Elise. Tetanus shots wouldn't have helped."

"If you two're gonna stand there arguing I'll go type this up for you to sign," Nick said, waving his little tape recorder.

"Bring our Pan back with you," Elise ordered. "I want to see if he'll rape Victor if I tell him to."

"Do you realize we're now making crude jokes about this?" Walters asked. "Are we so callous?"

"It's an indication you're recovering, now," Elise replied. "If you understand Lonnie didn't have anything to do with any of it and that the seduction and evil was all in your mind you're on the way to becoming human again. I'm afraid we do tend to lapse from our humanity when we approach the gods too closely."

"You scare the hell out of me when you talk like that," Nick said.

"I do? I can't fathom why."

"Because, all the evidence in this case – get the pun? – points to the strong probability you're right. Later!"

"My god!" Marsha cried as the tape recording ended. "That woman waltzes in there, makes him say, 'I'm sorry,' and that's the end of it? After he stabbed her three times!"

"She's a rather remarkable woman," Nick pointed out.

"This case really is something else!" Ed agreed. "I wouldn't like living in that neighborhood. No one's normal enough to fit any pattern."

"Oooohh, my *God*!" Marsha gasped, staring wide-eyed over Nick's shoulder.

"Nick?" Lonnie said, from behind him. "They told me I'd find you here."

Ed had a little smirk on his face, watching Marsha. Nick could see Shirley standing in the door behind, staring at Lonnie's back.

"Shouldn't you put on a shirt when you come in here?" Nick asked.

"I didn't have one with me. Did you go to see Mr. Walters?"

"Yeah, Lon. I'm having Marsha type it up so he can sign it now. Lonnie Micks, Marsha Blevins."

"Oooohhhh my *goddd*!" Marsha said.

"And that's Shirley Kiser in the doorway. Shirley, Lonnie," Ed introduced.

"My god! He *is* Pan!" Shirley cried. Lonnie blushed. Marsha said, "Ooohhh my goodddd!"

"Want to hear the tape Walters made about it, Lonnie?" Nick asked. "Until Marsha gets over her shock she's gonna be totally worthless for transcribing it, anyhow. Mrs. Norton wants me to take you to the hospital when I go back to have him sign it. You'll see why when you hear it. It's pretty clear."

Lonnie seemed oblivious to Marsha and Shirley staring at him. He slipped on the earphones and sat listening to the tape while Nick finished his case report. Ed sighed, went to the door, took Shirley's shoulders in his hands and marched her back out to the reception desk. Marsha looked at Nick and grinned.

When the tape was finished, Lonnie gave the recorder and earphones to Marsha, who was now back to normal, and came to Nick.

"Mrs. Norton doesn't really want me to rape him, does she?"

"Would you?"

"No. I don't think so. I mean, Mrs. Norton really does know what she's talking about, I suppose, but rape's against my rules, just Like married women."

Marsha laid her head on her desk. Nick grinned.

"Anyone else, I'd say it was a joke. Elise, I don't really know."

"You don't *think* so?" Marsha asked Lonnie.

"Well, if it was really important, and he said he wanted me to, I guess it would be all right, but then, that's not actually rape anymore, is it?" Lonnie said, winking at Nick. "Mrs. Norton wouldn't ask me to do anything wrong.

"Nick, you said on there Jon really does want me to take him to bed? Really? I mean, he's a good friend and he helped us, so I think I owe him that much if he really ... I mean, if it's important."

Marsha had her head on the desk again.

"Well, that part's up to you," Nick replied, turning so Marsha couldn't see he was about to have a laughing fit. "I mean with Jon. Walters probably wouldn't like it."

"I'll drop by the construction and tell Jon I'll sleep with him tonight on my way back," Lonnie suggested, keeping a straight face – with some effort. "Gee, I wish people who want me to bed them would just *tell* me! I never know when they're serious!

"Do *you* want to go to bed with me? I mean, it's okay, but tonight I guess I should sleep with Jon and tomorrow night I already promised Gloria and Irene I'd stay at their place. I'll have the next night free I think – or any afternoon. Well, most afternoons."

"Awright! Can it!" Marsha demanded. "You went too far with that one! This is getting me back for Paddy, right? I bait him, you bait me."

Nick and Lonnie let loose and howled. Paddy stepped out of his office door, looked around, stared at Lonnie a moment, and announced, "I can guess who *you* are! What in hell is going on out here? What's the noise?"

"Lonnie has just told Nick he couldn't make an appointment to screw him tonight or tomorrow night, but he would be free the following night or almost any afternoon," Marsha answered. "They had me going for a minute."

"Oh. Did you get Walters' statement?" Paddy asked, shaking his head. Marsha held up the tape and said that's what started it. Elise Norton said she wanted to see if Lonnie would rape Walters if she asked him to.

"He wouldn't have to rape him. That's what you said the whole thing was about," Paddy retorted. "I can see why he was so attracted to you.

"I'm Paddy James. These clowns don't have any manners or home training at all."

"I'll transcribe this and you can get Walters to sign it," Marsha said. "He'll plead involuntary manslaughter?"

"That's about it," Nick answered.

"Just involuntary manslaughter?" Lonnie asked. "What about Mrs. Norton?"

"She marched into his room to demand that he apologize for stabbing her three times," Nick replied. "He apologized, so that's all forgiven and forgotten."

Page 169

"Oh,"

"You're putting *me* on now, right?" Paddy asked, ready to either grin or get indignant, whatever the situation called for.

"No. That was the whole deal. He also has to pay for whatever the insurance doesn't of her hospital bills."

"Why are the people in your cases nutsville?!" Paddy cried. "Great gods of yore! First you know who the killers are and can't get proof, then you have the victims making plea deals with their attackers to get off! You're all crazy! You're as bad as they are!"

"You know, I always have thought the people there are sort of weird," Lonnie said. "That's why I fit in so well.

"I'll ride back to the hospital with you when you take the statement in if you don't mind, Nick. I want to talk to Mr. Walters. I said some things about him I shouldn't have."

"I thought you didn't have a shirt with you," Marsha said.

"I don't. Why?"

"They won't let you roam around in a hospital with no shirt or shoes!"

"They didn't say anything before," Lonnie said, confused.

Marsha put her head on her desk.

"Ha! Would *you* tell Lonnie to put on more clothes?" Nick asked.

"I don't want to hear it! I'll bet he lives in the woods – in a log cabin!" Marsha said into her desk pad.

"I built it myself!" Lonnie agreed, proudly. "I think it looks really natural there."

"Lonnie, where do you live? Really," Nick asked.

"Down off of Corkscrew. Out past the end. I have a twenty acre plot. I used some of the cypress to build my cabin when I thinned it. The place has room for me to grow all kinds of stuff and has some nice cypress and oaks and a nice pond with a stream."

"If you gambol around your place in the nude I think I'll die right here!" Marsha said. "I'll go hide in the bushes to watch, but I'll die!"

"I don't do that!" Lonnie replied, blushing. "Well, not very often. I mean, I've got dewberries and French briars."

Marsha laid her head back on her desk. Paddy stared with a sort of unbelieving half-grin.

Nick said, "I guess those thorns could get painful in the more tender areas. Let's take this to Walters."

Marsha asked, "Is that part true? That you don't sleep with married women?"

"That wouldn't be right," Lonnie said, simply.

"Damn! How 'bout if I get a divorce?" Marsha replied, with a grin. "Could you spare me a couple of hours then?"

"I don't think I believe in divorce. That's too much like breaking a promise. You shouldn't do that."

Paddy was staring at him in utter disbelief. Marsha couldn't decide whether to lay her head on the desk again or to cry.

Nick and Lonnie left.

Walters stared at Lonnie for a long minute, then turned toward Nick. "Excuse me? He wants to apologize to *me*!?"

"I said some things I shouldn't have said," Lonnie explained. "I go around telling people it's not right, then find myself doing it."

"You were merely reacting to the way I was acting. I never so much as returned a smile. I was afraid. I see I had no reason to be."

"Mrs. Norton explained that. I've never thought about it before, but I've read enough to know how the things your parents teach you can screw you up."

"Are your parents living, Lonnie?" Walters asked.

"No. Mom died in eighty two and Dad died about six months later. He didn't want to go on living without her, so he willed himself to die."

"They must have been truly wonderful people. You could be what I first thought you were if they'd been at all like my parents. The inner conflict between the superb physical appearance you've inherited and the idea of sin would destroy you."

"Mom and Dad always told me that I was going to be handsome. Dad was always really goodlooking, and so was Mom. Both of their families are, so it's logical I would be.

"Uncle Ben raised me from when they died. He's really the most handsome one. He taught me not to be arrogant or any of that, because it was going to cause a lot more problems than it solved.

"Aunt Dolly always taught me that there wasn't anything actually inherently evil, it's what we do with a thing that makes it good or bad. She told me people would want to look at me and touch me and even to sleep with me because I was a Micks.

"She said it was okay if I wanted them to, but I was never to go to bed with anybody I didn't want."

"Where were you raised?" Nick asked.

"In Tennessee. In the mountains. We were a pretty long way from anywhere. Our closest neighbors were over a mile away while I was growing up and more than a half mile after I went to live with Uncle Ben."

"Who educated you? I mean, where did you get your schooling?" Walters asked.

"I didn't go to formal school. Mom taught me math and reading. We had hundreds of books. I've always read everything I can get my hands on since I was seven or eight."

"No one to play with as a child?" Nick asked.

"Not very often."

"We're trying to figure you out," Walters explained. "Are you Irish or – you'd have to be. Micks."

"I'm three quarters Scotch and Irish," he said. "There's about a quarter Greek. The name was Miksoliateus or something, but my great grandfather three times removed couldn't spell it, so he was writing down M-I-K-S and stopped. The man at Ellis Island said it was spelled with a C and added it for him. We've been Micks ever since! Later, Gramps twice removed married a MacTavish and Gramps once removed married a McNish."

"You actually do know how you affect people, don't you?" Nick asked. "The 'who me?' innocent part's an act?"

"If you mean, do I know women want to bed me, Mom and Dad and everybody always told me that was going to happen. If you mean a lot of men would want to, Dad and Uncle Ben told me that would happen, too. They said I had to make all decisions about sex on my own.

"I don't know what you mean about any act. I don't know why they do, except that the Micks men are always handsome. I know I am, but I don't see why there's anything so special about it. It's not like something I worked for.

"I was taught I should never be self-conscious just because I'm handsome. Mom and Dad said everybody has to have a code to live by. The true worth of a person is in how he or she lives always within the code, not how they look.

"That's why I respect Mrs. Norton so much. She has a code and she lives within it. So do you, Nick."

"Nick told me even he might somehow be sexually attracted to you," Walters said. "Did you know that?"

"Yes. I listened to the tape. That's what I mean about the

code. He believes in always telling the truth. That's a very important part of his code."

"It's the difference in what he is and what I am," Walters agreed. "He's quite comfortable within himself and he doesn't have a lot of silly insecurities about what he might be. The idea of sin wasn't drummed into him when he was small.

"I have doubts about my feelings. I don't really know what I am or who I am – or didn't. I think I'm slowly learning.

"That's what this whole terrible thing was all along, wasn't it? Lonnie knows exactly who and what he is and he's completely comfortable with it. He likes himself. Nick is the same.

"I don't really know who or what I am. I see small glimpses of things at times and try to run away from them, but I must carry them with me. I am not comfortable with who and what I am.

"Nick said you've never slept with Le Bonne, but I think that you would if you thought it would help him in some way. I think you most probably would never think of it again after you did."

"Of course I would! Sex is as close as two people can ever be, in a way. I would never forget anyone I slept with! How can you forget sharing someone else's body?"

"Yes. Sharing. To you, sex is always sharing." It was a simple statement, not a question. "You share everything, while I share nothing.

"What about you, Nick?"

"I suppose I probably take more than I give back. Lonnie gives more than he takes. This was a tragic way for you to have to learn a simple fact, wasn't it?

"No two people are alike."

"I think I love life and sharing it. I wouldn't change a

thing from what I have now," Lonnie replied. "Nick is comfortable with his life. He wouldn't change his life very much. He shares most things. You aren't comfortable with your life and would change a lot. You were taught sharing was evil, so you're afraid to let yourself share."

"It's even simpler than that," Walters replied. "You don't fear anything much. Nick's fears are logical and realistic, according to what he does. I've always been afraid of life."

"You were taught to be," Nick said.

"Exactly! – and Lonnie and you were taught *not* to be. *That's* the big difference," Walters said, with a rueful look. "It's all in how you was brung up!"

"And there's the motive I wasn't sure I'd ever find," Nick agreed. "It's one of those simple kinds of things that are so complicated no one can fully understand them."

A nurse came in and asked Nick and Lonnie to leave (Making it plain with her eyes that Lonnie could ignore her if he liked. *She* certainly hoped he would!).

"We'll go see Mrs. Norton for a few minutes, okay?" Lonnie asked her.

"You can go anywhere you like," she replied, with a dreamy-eyed smile.

They found Elise preparing to call a taxi to take her home, so Nick said he'd be more than happy to give her a ride. They checked her out and he drove to the door to pick her up. Lonnie slid into the back seat and she sat next to Nick.

"Well! It was nice of you to come pick me up! How did you know I was checking out?"

Nick looked in the rearview mirror before telling her they were there to get Walters' statement signed. Lonnie grinned and winked.

"We really went to see Mr. Walters and came to see you when we were through. I couldn't do it the way you wanted. I tried."

"Do what, dear?"

"Rape Mr. Walters. Nick said you'd asked for me to, so I tried, but he just kept saying I couldn't rape a willing person and told me to get in the bed. I figured it would be the same thing, so what the hell?"

She didn't show a flicker. "Probably good for him. Now he knows."

"Knows what?" Lonnie asked, looking pretty uncertain.

"Why, whether he's gay or not. If he liked it, he is. If he didn't like it, he's not."

Nick caught *her* wik and said, "Oh, he liked it! The nurse had to come tell them to keep the thumping and grunting down. She didn't seem in the least surprised to find them like that."

"In bed?" Elise asked.

"Well, by then they were mostly out of the bed, but that's more or less what I meant."

"Ah-ha! So you're putting *me* on now!" Lonnie grinned. "It won't work, Nick. You don't lie, remember?"

"What's so special about this guy I have to see for my-self?" Janet, Nick's fiancee, asked as they drove out along Corkscrew Road. "All I hear around all you people is `Lonnie this' and `Lonnie that' – particularly from Marsh."

"I have to see this one dude!" Hank, Marsha's husband, said from the back seat. "I want to see if I get hot over him like Marsh says guys do."

"I didn't!" Nick said, slowing 'way down as they left the paved part of the road. "He said the going got tough out here, and he wasn't kidding!"

"*You* said you didn't really know for certain whether there was a sexual attraction or not!" Marsha accused. "Everybody knows that means there was!"

Marsha and Nick had been teasing each other mercilessly since Marsha had made the remark about how many smarts some guy must have who would actually introduce his girl to Lonnie.

"I want to see you `just die' if he's running around nude out there!" Nick said, with a smirk. "Will you really hide in the bushes to watch?"

"Ha! With *him* I'd just walk up, say `Hi!' and tackle him!" Marsha grinned.

"Running around nude?" Janet asked, with a sidewise look at Nick. "I hope he knows we're coming."

"No, he doesn't. I told him we'd come out sometime.

"I'll be damned! He actually did build one!" They could see a picturesque log cabin through a break in the cypress to their right. "How do we get to it?"

"There's a truck parked just ahead – and a path," Janet said. "Isn't this a beautiful place! Look at that huge iris bed! Are those spathiphyllums growing like that?"

"Oooohhh my *god*!" Marsha commented. "This place is so *lush*!"

"He's a part of nature, so nature responds," Nick said, as he parked next to Lonnie's truck. "Actually, he told me how to get plants to grow like that.

"I guess we have to walk in to the house."

"This is a lot like those botanical gardens we saw, isn't it, Marsh?" Hank asked. "I wish I'd brought the camcorder! What a showplace!"

"Do *not* mention camcorders!" Nick laughed. "There's a nice gravel path to the house."

They got out to stand staring at the scene for a moment, then moved silently (After Marsha said quietly, "I'm actually getting a little scared!") along the path toward the cabin. They were almost to the door when they heard laughter from around back, so moved around the cabin.

Lonnie was standing just outside the overhang of a huge water oak. Under the tree was an enormous bed of Nun's Orchids and Ladies Slippers. The bigger branches of the tree near the trunk were covered in orchids, bromeliads, rhipsalis, and other colorful epiphytes. Colorful plants were growing everywhere around in random beds, brilliant in color and delightful in fragrance. A small grass pond with a wide fringe of every imaginable color of water lilies was behind.

A bright band of sunlight came through the huge oak to shine on Lonnie, standing without a stitch of clothes, feeding a doe a handful of grass while a small fawn nibbled tender grass at his feet. There were white ibis and Muskovy ducks picking among the lush grass around the pond and within a couple of feet of Lonnie.

Suddenly, the doe turned to stare fixedly at them and the fawn followed her gaze. Lonnie turned, smiled broadly and threw open his arms to cry, "Welcome to Olympus!"

Nick sat bolt upright in bed.

Damn it! He, Janet, Marsha and Hank were driving out to Lonnie's this morning, then they were going to take Jim Hill's boat out to the barrier island for a relaxing day of fishing and picnicking. Lonnie told Nick to drop by anytime and how to get to his place – and he *didn't* know they were coming!

How *did* Lonnie affect him? That there was a strong impact was undeniable. That he liked him was obvious, too. That there were strong sexual implications in *that* dream couldn't be denied, either, but was it the fear of Janet responding to Lonnie like he knew she would or *was* he really attracted, sexually? He decided what he really feared was that Janet would react to Lonnie the same as any other woman. He wouldn't be too bothered by that and Lonnie would act like Lonnie always acted. The women could all moon over him. He wouldn't notice.

Nick shook his head and looked at the clock. It was time to get up anyhow, so he did.

He slipped out of bed, carefully, so as not to awaken Janet and plodded into the bathroom. When he came back Janet was awake. She smiled and said, "I like you all tousled like that! It's so natural, somehow. I don't think Marsha would rant about your Pan so much if she ever saw you like that!"

"If Marsha ever saw me like this you'd already have something to worry about. Now get up, woman! We have to go calling on Pan!"

"Ha-ah! I wouldn't have a thing to worry about with Marsha!" Janet laughed. "She wouldn't mess around on Hank! I'm not so sure about *you*, though!"

"Ha! Just look at it like a detective. If she saw me like this she'd *already* be messing around on Hank!"

Janet laughed again and threw a pillow at him, then

climbed out of bed. She went into the bathroom while Nick slipped on a robe and went to start breakfast.

If they drove out there and came to that path leading to that log cabin he was going to use the little lot by the truck to turn around and he was going to get the hell out of there! Simply because he was the luckiest guy in the world didn't mean he was going to push it!

C. D. Moulton's works are available on most major outlets as printed or e-books. CD writes the CD Grimes, PI, mysteries, the Det. Lt. Nick Storie mysteries, the Clint Faraday mysteries, the Flight of the Maita science fiction series, books on orchid culture and many others of many types. Mystery, adventure, intrigue, science fiction, humor, fantasy, paranormal, mild erotica, and factual.